Not Another Love Story

By

Autumn La'Dawn

EllaSoul Productions

EllaSoul Productions

Take a walk in the shoes of Alani, a brown-skinned, heavy-duty cutie who thought she had it all. Alani has a great life with a man she's been with since grade school and a booming business. But when her man can't keep it together, her picture-perfect life starts to unravel. She soon realizes that you can't keep a man that doesn't want to be kept.

Khan loves Alani, but he can't seem to remain exclusive to her. Every time he tries to do right by her, he fucks up again. Will he fuck up one too many times for her liking?

Alani has given Khan chance after chance to do right by her, only for him to continuously mess up. The only thing she wants from him is loyalty, but it seems as if she is asking for too much. She then must stop and ask herself: How much can one heart take?

Bam and Alani are best friends and virtually inseparable. Bam has some skeletons in her closet that not even Alani knows about. When getting into a relationship with Khan's cousin and right-hand

3

man, Rock, she realizes that she won't be able to keep her demons under wraps for too much longer.

Will Bam push Rock into the arms of another woman? Will Rock be there for Bam when she needs him most or will their relationship dry up like a raisin in the sun? Walk with Alani and Khan in a whirlwind romance as lies are told and loyalty is tested. Can a decade-long relationship weather the storm or will it all fall by the wayside? This is Not Another Love Story.

EllaSoul Productions

Chapter 1

Alani

♫ Am I wrong for thinking that we could be something so real? ♫

I woke up to the sounds of my ringing phone. Irritated that my sleep was being interrupted, I checked the time on the alarm clock and it was a little past 3am. I rolled over and grabbed my phone and answered without checking to see who was calling.

"Hello," I answered the phone, grumpily.

"Is that how you answer the phone for your man," replied Khan, my long-term boyfriend.

An instant smile popped up on my face. I should've known it was him from the ringtone. Khan and I had been together since middle school and I loved this man with every fiber of my being. In my eyes, Khan could do no wrong and vice versa. I was his princess and he was my prince. We met when I was a little short, fat girl with glasses, small breasts, and a huge ass that all the boys, and sometimes even grown men, drooled over. Other than the cat calls that I would receive from my rather big rear end, I got no play back then.

5

Anybody that wanted to talk to me was Usually fat and ugly... until I met Khan. He swooped in like a white knight and took me under his wing. It's been a wrap for us since then. In my young eyes, he was the best thing since sliced bread.

"I'm sorry baby, I didn't know it was you. But you know I don't play when it comes to my sleep."

I needed my beauty rest and Khan knew this, so I was at a loss as to why he would be calling my phone this late.

"Is something wrong, Bae?" I asked immediately going into defense mode.

"No baby, I just wanted to talk to you. I needed to hear your voice," he replied.

Shit like this made me love my man more and more each day. It's always been the little things that he did that kept a smile on my face.

"Aww, Bae. I love you," I said.

"I love you too, baby. I want to see you," he told me.

I was at my mother's house because we liked to spend at least one weekend out of the month with each other. She'd kept my room just as I'd left it when I moved into my own home with Khan.

EllaSoul Productions

"Well come get me from my Mama's house. I'll be ready when you get here," I told him before ending the call.

I hopped out of the bed and walked to the personal bathroom in my room. I stepped out of my clothes to take a quick shower. After I set the water to an appropriate temperature, I stopped in front of the full-length mirror to just admire my beauty.

I'd come a long way from the girl that I used to be, and I loved every inch of my curvy frame. I weighed 210 pounds. Some would call me fat, but I considered myself a plush pal. I toned that 210 pounds up and feel damn good about the way I looked. When the boobs and the butt make you ignore the gut, that's the definition of thick. And I'm thick in all the right places.

Gone were the glasses, replaced by a pair of contacts. My natural eye color was a light brown, which was shielded by my glasses once upon a time. I had a predominately flat stomach and toned legs. My skin was the same color as caramel and my hair stopped just past my shoulders with honey blonde highlights. I also kept a fresh Peruvian or Brazilian bundle in my shit.

I'm a certified bombshell; I'm bad and I know it. There wasn't anything a bitch or nigga could tell me to make me think otherwise. Upon realizing I'd been standing in the mirror admiring

7

my naked frame for about ten minutes, I hopped in the shower. After scrubbing my body three times with my favorite Bath and Body Works body wash, Pink Chiffon, I decided that it was time to get out. I cut off the water and stepped out of the shower. I threw my hair into a messy bun and went to find something to throw on. My baby was coming to get me, and knowing him, he probably had something up his damn sleeve.

EllaSoul Productions

Chapter 2

Khan

Khan /kan/

The ruler or leader

When I woke up, I knew I'd fucked up big time. I knew my bitch's scent like the back of my hand and this wasn't it, in addition to the cheap weave laying on the pillow beside me, giving it all away. How could I fall asleep over this bitch Brooke's house? I knew if/when wifey found out she was going to kill me. I hopped up out of the bed and scrambled to find my clothes, wallet, and phone. I had no missed calls from my girl so that was a good thing.

She most likely wasn't sweating me because she wasn't home herself. Being that she was at her mom's crib, I was good, but I still didn't want to be here. The worst thing you can ever do is fall asleep at a thot's house. That bitch can do or be up to anything. She can take pictures of your ass and send them to your bitch or anything else she wants to when you're asleep.

I had a banging headache, so I went in the bathroom to get some pain pills and take a leak. I knew I shouldn't have gone to the club with my niggas last night. I remember us smoking some granddaddy Kush on the way there and drinking on

9

some Hennessey like it was water. I was in my zone, vibing to the music when this bitch Brooke came up behind me and started grinding on me. When I turned around and saw it was her, I almost pushed her ass.

She knew neither me nor my bitch fucked with her like that. They had bad blood although it never came to blows, and it was all because of me. I'd fucked Brooke a couple of times, but she was a roller and I just couldn't wife her. This hoe just refused to get the picture. I admit I led her on in the past, but I had since told her that there wasn't shit popping off between us. Anything we could've had was dead and done.

What made it worse was that she was best friends with my sister, Khanna. I slipped up a couple times and cheated on wifey with her, but I told Alani that it was just because she was jealous of her, which was true. My girl has never left me over the accusations Brooke has thrown out there, so I would say that it's safe to assume that she's always believed my lies.

Brooke had some good pussy, but she ain't have shit on my Princess. I was her first everything and the only one who had been up in that gushy. I met Brooke back in the day, a couple months before I met Alani. We chilled a couple times and I just couldn't vibe with her. So when I met Alani, she

10

was my breath of fresh air. I remember that day like it was yesterday.

I was walking down the hallway in school with my cousins Chino and Rock.

"Damn bruh, that bitch got a fat ass I'm bouta try and get that," my cousin told me, eyeing her lustfully.

I told him to go ahead.

"Ayoo," Chico called out to her.

When she turned around and I caught a glimpse of her face, I knew she was heaven sent. She had her hair in a messy bun that I grew to love and bangs that she constantly pushed out of her face to stop them from blocking her glasses. Now, all I had to do was see how she carried herself when my cousin tried to holla at her. I couldn't do anything with a girl that anybody could get.

My cousin wasn't ugly, but he wasn't me.

She turned her nose up at my cousin and kept walking.

"You ugly anyways, bitch," Chino yelled.

"Fuck you, nigga. See a bitch, smack a bitch, fuck boy," Alani screamed back to Chino.

Her best friend, Bam came out of nowhere and pushed him down the stairs that were less than

11

two feet away from where they were standing. Bam was a straight up cutthroat; my cousin sprained his ankle and broke his arm that day.

I needed somebody like her by my side. She ain't even look like she was built like that, but then again, those were the ones that you had to watch out for. I'd made it my mission to get her. I loved the fact that she had a savage ass attitude but had a sweet and innocent look to her.

"Bitch, you done lost your fucking mind coming up on me," I growled.

"I know you miss me, daddy. That bitch La'La can't be doing her job right 'cause you always come running back," she replied with a smirk

"Don't you ever disrespect my girl again in your life or you won't have one," I said in her ear while squeezing her arm.

"I'm sorry, Khan. Let me go," she said with a look of fear on her face.

I let her go and started to walk away. Then, the DJ started playing "Body Party" by Ciara. She took that as her cue to grab me and to push her ass up on me and start winding her body on my dick. I tried to push her off to no avail. I was drunk and high as fuck, so I just stood there watching her give the whole club a show. She had no class about her. The dress she wore was so short that you could see

EllaSoul Productions

all her best assets, along with the fact that she wore no panties.

I'm a nasty nigga and I have no qualms about it, so I put my hand up under her dress and stuck two fingers inside of her. Brooke loved that nasty shit, so all she did was start twerking on my dick even harder. I pulled my fingers and did a smell check. If that pussy was stank, then she wasn't getting shit from me but a "fuck you and have a nice day".

Some people even started recording us and snapping pictures. My dick was so hard, and I was so drunk that I threw out all my better judgment and snatched her up and took her to the restroom in the back of the club.

I locked the bathroom door and pushed her up against the sink.

"Bend that ass over bitch," I growled, and she obliged with a smile on her damn face.

I put a rubber on and began to pound in and out of her relentlessly. It was nothing but a fuck, and I wanted her to know that. She started screaming.

"Fuck me daddy! Oh, I missed this dick."

I ain't wanna' hear none of the shit coming from her mouth, so I shut that shit down quickly.

"Shut up bitch! This what you wanted, right?"

13

She nodded and whimpered, "Yes," while trying to muffle her moans.

I felt myself about to bust so I pulled out, snatched the condom off, and came all over her ass. Her hoe ass liked that freaky shit. I adjusted my pants and walked out the bathroom leaving her ass there. I went and found my boys and they instantly started clowning me. Rock, my younger cousin by a year, was always my voice of reason.

"Bruh, you know if Alani find out lil' sis gone paint this city red," Rock said.

I always valued Rock's opinion, but right now he was telling me some shit that I already knew. My girl is as thorough as they come and by far the realist bitch on my team. Well, her and her best friend, Bam.

"I know bruh, I don't need your mother fucking ass telling me 'I told you so'," I snapped at him. "I'm about to go holla' at Brooke real quick and kick her some dough so she'll keep her fucking mouth closed."

With that, I walked off to search through the club to find Brooke, which was kind of hard being that the club was packed.

Eventually, I found her on the dance floor dry fucking some scrub ass nigga, like she wasn't just bent over in the bathroom. I snatched her up and walked her towards the door.

"Fuck is wrong with you my nigga?" The scrub had the nerve to ask me.

I just looked at the nigga, but before I could respond, my nigga Mont came from thin air and slept the nigga. I just shook my head and walked away. I signaled to Rock who was sitting by the bar that I was out. I had to go see my baby after I finished up with Brooke; I needed to be near her. It's crazy how whenever I fucked up, instead of distancing myself from La'La, I tried to be closer to her.

"Bitch, let me tell you something and I'm going to make this real clear. There is nothing going on between us and there never will be. You leave me and mine alone before I have you taking a permanent dirt nap. If I have to repeat myself, you'll regret it," I sneered in her ear so that nosey bystanders wouldn't hear me.

Instead of heeding my warning, she kissed me and grabbed my semi-hard dick. I pulled back and walked her to my car. We rode in silence to her house for the first five minutes, then I said, "Suck my dick."

She obliged, pulled it out, and started working me over. Yeah, I know that I should've either just

EllaSoul Productions

carried my ass home or back into the club. But like Kevin Gates said:

I'm just thinking with my dick!

Brooke was slurping and spitting all on my shit, driving me crazy. Her pussy wasn't all that, but her fucking head game was the dumbest. She had all eleven and a half inches of my dick in her mouth, deep throating me. I had to stop her to keep from crashing my car. When we reached her house, it was a panties off situation. Well, it would have been if she had on any.

I tried to regain some of my composure, so I sat on the couch, but she straddled me. I pushed her off and told her to make me a drink and she stomped off to the kitchen. She came back into the living room wearing nothing but her heels and carrying two glasses. My dick shot up instantly. See now, Brooke wasn't an ugly girl, but she wasn't pretty either. She had a big nose that kind of made her look like a pig. She had a banging body, but she was a little on the chubby side. I took the cup out of her hand and downed the whole thing, then followed suit with the other. I knew I needed to be drunker than I was to bang her ass. She grabbed my hand and walked me to her bedroom. Everything else was a fog.

After I finished relieving myself, I washed my hands and sat on the toilet contemplating

16

my next move. I knew I couldn't stay here, I had to call Alani.

EllaSoul Productions

Chapter 3

Brooke

♫ Leave your lover, leave her for me ♫

I had Khan right where I wanted him. I knew he couldn't resist me. I felt him get out of the bed, but I acted like I was still sleeping. I heard him in the bathroom talking to that bitch Alani. I hated that bitch's guts. I had Khan first and I deserved to be with him. I knew I wasn't the prettiest girl, but I had a nice body and I wasn't a bum bitch. I just needed Khan to realize that I was the one for him and not her.

We all went to the same school and I was best friends with his sister, Khanna. She and I were thick as thieves and she hated Alani as much as I did, if not more. I was the only person she wanted to be with her brother. So, when I got the chance to get with him, I jumped at the opportunity. I'd always thought that he was fine as fuck. After a short period of messing around, and because we never had a title, he told me he didn't want shit to do with me. A couple days later, I found out through Khanna that he was with Alani. She sent me a picture of them together at her mother's monthly Sunday dinner. From that day on, I knew that I had to get him back and years later, I'm still not giving up. That's why I drugged his drink at my house.

18

I got my degree in Lurkology, so while stalking his Instagram, I saw that he and his niggas would be at the club. I picked up some roofies from some white guy I knew from out Chesapeake. I knew it would be easy to get him back to the crib and I succeeded in my mission.

He might think that we just so happened to be at the same club, but I only went because I knew he was going to be there with his crew. I pulled some thot wear out of my closet and hopped my ass in the shower. I made sure to douche my pussy twice, because I knew he wouldn't be able to resist me once I pushed up on him.

I was going to have my man by any means necessary. I still didn't know how he woke up that fast after all the fucking we did. Even though he pissed me off by calling me that bitch's name.

Soon after, I heard his car start up and pull out of my drive way. I got up and checked my phone. I got on Instagram and saw someone had posted and tagged me in a picture of Khan and me at the club. The wheels in my head immediately started turning. I quickly took a screenshot of the photo and posted it on my Instagram, tagging Alani and her ratchet ass best friend Bam in it. I hated her ass too.

Next, I called Alani. I'd gotten her number out of Khan's phone while he was sleeping

19

and saved it in mine under "Home Wrecker". I called, and she answered after three rings.

"Hello," I said to her with sass in my voice.

"Who is this?" The stuck-up bitch had the nerve to ask.

"You know who this is. I was just calling to let you know that our man is on his way over to you," I snickered.

"Brooke, you are so fucking pathetic. Stop playing on my phone and get you some business. You know good and god damn well that Khan doesn't want your big, sloppy ass. Bitch, get your life together and have several fucking seats," Alani yelled before she hung right up in my face. I swear, I was gone fuck this bitch up and be sitting pretty, right by Khan's side.

After all, I've put in a lot of work to have this man in my life. I need Khan more than I need the air I breathe. Within him, I lost myself. Without him, I found myself wanting to be lost again.

EllaSoul Productions

Chapter 4

Bam

♫ Baby girl my sister

Better off my best friend

Cuz if I pop off on a nigga bet she jumpin in ♫

I heard my phone ringing in my sleep and automatically knew it was my right hand La'La because of the assigned ringtone. We both had Gucci Mane's *Candy Lady* remix set for each other. Knowing it had to be something wrong with my girl, I picked up the phone with the quickness.

"What up, bitch? Do I need to suit up or what?" I asked all in one breath.

"Bitch, why the fuck did Brooke's big foot ass just call me talking about "our man is on his way home to you"? Girl, I'm so sick of this bitch," La'La told me in frustration.

"I know you didn't just take what that bitch had to say for face value. You know she been after Khan for years now," I told my longtime friend/sister.

"That's what I would've said if it wasn't for the fact that Khan had just called me twenty minutes

21

prior saying he was on his way to get me from my mama's house," she said.

I sighed, picking up my iPad and checking Instagram and Facebook. I loved Khan like the brother I never had, but I loved my sister La'La more and he knew I would end his ass for fucking with her heart.

Me and Alani weren't blood related, but she was the closest thing I've ever had to a sister. We were both only children and we'd been besties since grade school. I stopped listening to my sister, zoned out, and started seeing red until I heard her yelling my name.

"Bitch go on Instagram and check the picture that Brooke stank ass just posted."

I was staring at a picture of Khan grinding all on Brooke in Club Posh. My sister told me that she was going to call me back, so I knew that I had to get to Mama Angeline's house, and quick.

I knew Alani better than she knew herself, so I was more than sure that she was ready to set some shit off. I wasn't going to try to stop her because Khan was more than wrong, but I did need to be there for whatever was going to pop off.

I'm going to ride for my sister right, wrong, or indifferent. Now I'll tell her when she's wrong,

22

but at the same time, I'm still right behind her on the front line ready to rock when she rolls.

EllaSoul Productions

Chapter 5

Alani

Pissed off couldn't even be used to describe how I was feeling right now. I couldn't believe that Khan would embarrass and disrespect me like that by being in public with a bitch who couldn't stand me although the feeling was mutual. I was gon' fuck his trifling ass up. I was too through with him and this dusty bitch. I mean, a hoe gon' be a hoe, but my nigga is supposed to be loyal. Fuck all that other shit. Khan was going to make me stab his ass up something decent.

I've put up with a lot of shit from him throughout our relationship, but there comes a time when you have to step back and ask yourself is any of this shit even worth it. I know for a fact that I'm too good of a woman to be treated like shit, especially by a man that claims to love me. Pain surged through my body like a dagger to the heart, but I refused to allow any tears to fall. Then, my pain turned into rage.

I had an itch to fuck something up and that itch needed to be scratched. I might as well start with the person that was responsible for making me feel this way.

My thoughts were interrupted by my ringing phone. I knew it was his dirty ass by the ringtone. It

24

was Erykah Badu and Stephen Marley's song *In Love with You*, but right now I hated his ass.

"What!" I snapped into the phone letting my emotions get the best of me.

"Damn, Bae! You knew I was coming. What's wrong? I'm outside."

I hung up the phone ready to fire his ass up. I grabbed my favorite gun, a pearl handle baby Ruger 9mm, and went outside. He looked good as ever leaning against his car. He was six-foot-three with Hennessey colored skin, and the prettiest, straightest, and whitest teeth that I'd ever seen on a man. My baby could've been a Colgate model. He smiled that dimpled smile that I loved so much and under the street light I could see his dreads that I'd just re-twisted and braided back into two fishtails, and that he had went to get a line-up. And even the line-up was done to perfection. He was rocking some midnight black Robin jeans with the matching black and red shirt, topping it all off with a black and red bomber jacket.

I could smell his Hugo Boss cologne before I even got within arms' reach of him, which just so happened to also be my favorite scent for him to wear. But we weren't here for recreation, I was about to tear him a whole new asshole.

"Hey baby."

25

WHAP!

I smacked the shit out of his ass.

"What was that for?" He yelled.

WHAP!

I smacked his ass again, but this time, he held my wrist and growled in ear, "Don't hit me again, La'La, I done already told you about that shit. Keep your fucking hands to yourself!"

I knew he was serious because of the look in his eyes so I backed down, but only a little bit.

"I know you weren't over there fucking with that thot bitch, Brooke, Khan. You've got to be fucking shitting me," I screamed at him.

He started to speak but I cut him off. He knew I was serious when I called him Khan instead of "Bae". I was beyond hurt and fucking confused as to why he felt the need to constantly disrespect me. Now I'm far from a dumb bitch, but I love Khan and I couldn't picture life without him. He was my first everything. The one I gave my virginity to and I someday wanted to carry his kids. I knew he could possibly be fucking around with bitches from time to time, but why he would fuck with Brooke was beyond me.

She'd been labeled as a hoe for as long as I could remember, but that was the bitch my nigga decided he wanted to fuck with.

"Let me explain baby," he finally spoke up. I just stared at him with my hands on my hips and hatred in my eyes. "I know it looks bad, but I wasn't fucking with that broad, you got to believe me. You know how bad that bitch wants me, I wouldn't do you like that. I love you. You know you're my life and I would never do anything to jeopardize what we have."

He was laying on the charm, flashing me that million-dollar dimpled smile I loved so much. It was hard for me not to believe him when I knew how that bitch got down. He pulled me into his embrace and kissed my forehead just as my ace Bam was pulling up.

Bam and I go way back and I loved her like a sister. No fuck that, she is my sister. Bam's real name is Sophie, but I gave her the nick name Bam when we were younger because she was always strong like Bam Bam from the Flintstones.

We'd been tight since the sandbox and I didn't see anything changing that. I trusted Bam with my life and she trusted me with hers. I would ride on any bitch for fucking with my hitta. She hopped out the car with it still running, almost forgetting to put it in park. She jumped up to slap

27

Khan in the back of his head and then started going in on his ass.

"Fuck is wrong with your disrespectful ass, bruh?" she asked him. He just stood there looking at us like we were crazy. "Oh, so you wanna act stupid now?"

She reached in the car, pulled out her phone, and went to Instagram. I could tell by the change in his demeanor that she'd shown him the picture that Brooke had tagged us in. I knew he was getting mad because of the protruding vein in his forehead and the fact that he was clenching his jaw.

He finally spoke.

"Sis I just told her the same thing I'm about to tell you. That shit ain't what it seem. I knew that snake bitch was up to something," he sneered

"Well I'm up to something, too," Bam snickered.

That's when I noticed that she had on all-black clothing and a pair of black Timbs with her hoodie on. She was ready to scrap. You could always count on Bam to not even know the situation and be ready for whatever.

"Show me where this ditzy bitch live 'cause I'mma fuck her up since she think it's okay to fuck with my sis."

EllaSoul Productions

Khan looked at me, but we both knew that when Bam had a taste for blood there was nothing that anybody could do about it. Point. Blank. Period. We all hopped inside of Khan's car and rode out to Brooke's house in silence.

Nothing but the sounds of the radio filled the car as we all sat, lost in our own thoughts. I didn't know what was plaguing their minds, but mine was filled with thoughts of Khan. The man that I missed even when we were sleeping right next to each other. The man that held the key to my heart. The man that I'd always thought could do no wrong. The man that I'd always thought so highly of. The man that is supposed to be the father of my future children, was also the man that had broken my heart, yet again.

EllaSoul Productions

Chapter 6

Khan

♫ You better put that that woman first ♫

When I pulled up to see Alani, the last thing on my mind was that this bitch Brooke had pulled some crazy shit. I didn't think my actions were going to bite me in my ass this quick. But karma was a bad bitch, and she never missed an appointment. Now I was just hoping that this broad didn't say shit to my girl to further incriminate me. The light was on in the living room, so I knew that she was up. But the problem I was having was that my sister, Khanna's, car was in the driveway. I didn't want my girl, my sister, Brooke, and Bam who was just like my sister, to get into it, especially because it was all my damn fault.

Bam was the first one out the car. She was trigger happy and that's why she was on my team... but I knew it was about to be some shit when we went up in this house.

"Alright Khan, you gone go up to the door and knock on it and I'mma bust up in that bitch," Bam said.

"Alright, but y'all leave Khanna alone. I know she's messy too, but that's my sister. I don't give a fuck what you do to Brooke," I replied shaking my head.

I knew that there was absolutely nothing that I could do about it. I took the three steps up to the porch, regretting all my decisions up to this moment. I didn't know how I let my man down stairs cloud my better judgment. I loved Alani and I knew she was going to be my wife one day. I just had to get and stay on my shit and start doing right by her. I'd told her on numerous occasions that I didn't deserve her. She needed to be with a standup guy, someone who would do right by her and keep her safe.

But she insists that I'm the only nigga she wants to be with and that she couldn't picture her life with anybody else.

I knocked on the door and looked at Brooke as she peeked through the window. The bitch had the nerve to start smiling when she saw me, like this was a social call or some shit.

As soon as she opened the door she said, "Hey Boo! Back so..." was all she got out before Bam kicked her and Alani's way in.

"What the fuck, Khan?!" My sister yelled.

"Fuck all that, you sleazy bitch. Keep trying to fuck with my man" Alani smirked and punched Brooke right in her face.

Brooke's nose burst instantly, and Khanna jumped up to hit Alani. Then, Bam dropped her ass and started pounding her face in. All the while,

31

Alani was dragging Brooke by her weave and beating her in her face. Figuring it was time to break it up, I scooped Alani and Bam up kicking and screaming, and took them to the car.

"Don't fucking move" I told them sternly and they obliged.

I went back into the house to check on my sister, fuck Brooke's ass.

"Khan how the hell you gone let them come in here and do us like that?" Khanna screamed at me.

I didn't say anything as I helped her off the floor and found a first aid kit to tend to her wounds. I loved my sister, but she was just as messy and ratchet as her damn friend, and that's what made me want to keep my damn distance. After I finished up with my sister, I kissed her forehead and went to leave.

"Khan, I'm going to make sure you and them bitches pay for this and I'mma make you wish you never met me or broke my heart," Brooke said, as I opened the door. I'll never forget those words and the pain behind them.

I usually didn't pay that hoe any mind, but for some reason, I felt as if she would make good on her promise.

Chapter 7

Khanna

Fed up

"Bitch don't threaten my brother. You're my sister and all but you already know how I am. I don't play when it comes to him. Fuck them other bitches," I snapped on her ass. I got up to go check my face out in the mirror. I still couldn't believe what had just gone down. How my brother could let those bitches come in here in beat us down like that was beyond me.

I couldn't stand those hoes. Brooke was the only person that I wanted my brother to be with once upon a time. But this pointless feud with Alani and Bam had to come to an end, and soon. I didn't know how much more I could take. Bam had put a big ass knot on my head, my lip was busted, I had tiny scratches all over my face, and I noticed a bruise forming on my right cheek bone.

I was too pretty to be walking around with my face fucked up. I went back into the living room to clean up the broken glass and turned over furniture. There was a broken lamp, the glass coffee table was broken, and all the pictures had been knocked off wall, leaving glass in their place.

I needed to sit down and talk to Brooke because I couldn't keep going on like this. She was

33

always doing some dumb shit to break-up Alani and Khan, but damn, it had been ten fucking years now, enough was enough. I felt like it was time to let go of her little hoop dreams, but not for Brooke. She just refused to stop. She would mess with other men from time to time, but she never entertained a relationship with them, because in her head, Khan was going to come around one day.

"I think that you should just let him go. It's been long enough and it's obvious that he's not leaving her. No matter how many times you throw the pussy at him, he's still just going to look at you like a quick fuck," I said giving it to her straight with no chaser.

"Girl boo, he loves me and can't get enough of me. That's why he keeps coming back for more. I just need to help him get her out of his system. She has her claws sunk into him so deep it's hard for him to just pull away without losing a piece of himself in the process," she said matter-of-factly while holding ice to her busted lip.

This bitch was dumber than I thought. She must be delusional to believe the shit that just spilled out of her mouth.

"Yeah, and if he leaves her, the piece of himself that he'll be losing is his heart because she has it and there is nothing you can do about it," I

EllaSoul Productions

told her trying to get her to see that her efforts were futile.

"Child, please. He may be with her, but I can guarantee you he is always thinking about me. They may have been together for the last ten years, but he has also been with me for the last ten years. So what does that make her?" Brooke asked stupidly.

"It makes her blindly in love, but it also makes you a home wrecking side hoe. You act like she's sleeping with your man when it's definitely the other way around. She hasn't done shit to you besides snatch up the man that you want. The way I see it, the best woman won and you need to bow out and accept defeat gracefully."

I didn't even bother to wait for her to respond. I gathered my shit, hopped in my car, and rode off. She had me rethinking our entire friendship. Birds of a feather flock together and I was nothing like her ass. I'd never seen a dove chilling with a pigeon.

EllaSoul Productions

Chapter 8

Alani

After the ass whooping we put on Brooke and Khanna I was hungry, so we all decided to head to the Waffle House for a bite to eat. After ordering our food, I felt as if I needed to speak on the events that had just transpired.

"So babe, I know you're probably mad at us and shit, but you know they had it coming. Your sister has never liked me, but I think that it's so distasteful to encourage her friend to still try and get with you. Honestly, you need to talk to her because I might not be as merciful next time. I'm sick of this shit. If it ain't one thing it's another," I vented.

I could see the look of contemplation on his face as he sat, staring intently into space. Sister or no sister, I would end that bitch. Bam spoke up seeing as Khan was still contemplating.

"Well it they didn't start it then we wouldn't have had to finish it. I'm so sick of them hoes as well."

Finally, Khan spoke up and said, "I know my sister isn't a saint, but I'm going talk to her, alright. Because I can't have my wife and sister in-law beefing with my sister. But what if she say she wants to have a sit down with y'all, is that something that y'all would agree to? Because I'm not up for no bullshit. Fuck Brooke, I just don't want y'all to try and beat my sister's ass again."

I thought about it for a split second then responded.

"I mean if them bitches ain't on no dumb shit, I ain't got no problem with it."

I looked to Bam and she nodded her head in agreement.

Our food arrived and we all ate in silence for a few minutes.

"Well, you know my mama has her monthly Sunday dinner coming up. I don't see why we can't do it then," Khan said out of nowhere

He knew that I always went to Mama Megan's Sunday dinners, but he also knew that I wouldn't disrespect her house by fighting. He thought he was slick, but I had to applaud him for his efforts. He knew that was a sure way to make sure Bam and I acted right.

We finished up our food, paid the tab, left a hefty tip, and headed back to drop Bam off at her car. I was in the car with them, but my mind was somewhere else. I knew Khan was lying through his damn teeth. He must think I'm stupid, but ain't nothing slick to a can of oil. I could show him better

37

than I could tell him that I ain't the bitch to be fucked with. But he should know that by now.

EllaSoul Productions

Chapter 9

Alani

Calling a Truce

So here we were at my mother in-law's house. Mama Megan was a force to be reckoned with. She was what you called, honest to a fault, but that's what everybody loved about her. The tension in the room was so thick you could cut it with a knife. Everybody was eating but nobody was talking. Then, I guess Mama Megan couldn't take it no more so she spoke.

"I'm sick of y'all motherfuckers and this dumb ass shit y'all got going on."

We all knew better than to cut her off, well I thought we all did.

"But ma," Brooke attempted to say.

"Shut the fuck up, especially you. Since when did it become okay to try and keep a man that don't want to be kept? You keep chasing after some dick and then want to make up excuses as to why you keep going back. He has a girl and you need to boss the fuck up and accept it. And you, Khanna. I don't care who the fuck you want to be with your brother, you don't encourage nobody to try and take somebody else's man. He's obviously happy where the fuck he is so drop it. You and Brooke need to stop being so messy.

"Khan, you need to keep that fucking dirty ass dick of yours in your fucking pants. You gone fuck around and lose a good girl doing all this dumb shit. I ain't raise you to treat nobody like shit, so you need to get your shit together. La'La, I know you love my son, but don't be stupid over his ass. If he can't get his shit together, drop his simple ass like a bad fucking habit because he knows better. Bam, I don't even have no words for your crazy ass. You just need to chill your hot-headed ass out. I'm so sick of y'all and your pointless drama. Now, I'm about to go get me something to drink and smoke my blunt while y'all talk this shit out. There better not be any fighting or yelling in my damn house, so act like you got some damn sense."

And with that, she walked off.

We all sat in silence, letting her words sink in. We had all just gotten read by Mama Megan. Nobody dared argue their point because we all knew everything that she had said was dead on. All this feuding was bad for business. We needed to be worried about outsiders trying to take us out, not our families. So, I knew that we had to tighten up, and quick.

The silence was killing me; it was so quiet in the room you could hear a mouse piss on a cotton ball. So, I took this as my moment to speak up.

"Look, Brooke, other than you trying to fuck with my nigga, I ain't got no problem with you. Now don't get me wrong, I'm not just blaming you 'cause this nigga know better, but at the end of the day, I'll kill for mine, best believe that. So, if you got a problem staying the fuck away from him, let me know now."

I sat there staring at her daring her to say something slick, but it never came. I'd go to war for my nigga without question whether he's right, wrong, or indifferent. I'd never been the type of person to leave someone I love out to dry, especially my man. Khan fucked up more than a lil' bit, but that's the love of my life, and I didn't put in all this work with him for it to be in vain. I wasn't going to leave my man for some hoe that popped her pussy for the biggest baller in a five-mile radius.

As I stared in Brooke's direction, I couldn't ignore the undeniable look of sadness she had etched on her face. At the end of the day, I was a woman first and if I'd ever had my heart broken, I would at least want some closure. Whether he wanted to or not, he was going to have to go and talk to her. In some crazy way, I felt bad for her. Having your heart broken is a pain that no medicine could heal.

41

The only time that you get relief from a broken heart was when you fall asleep. But when you wake up and your eyes fall on your tear-stained pillow and the trashcan full of tissue that was used to wipe your eyes, the pain you felt comes rushing back. Missing somebody causes everything to remind you of them and suddenly the bad times didn't seem so bad.

I pulled out my iPhone 6 plus and texted Khan, telling him he needed to pull her outside and talk to her. He looked over at me after reading the message and I shot him a look telling him that I wasn't fucking playing.

"Brooke, let me holla at you real quick," Khan said to her as he stood up and headed towards the back patio door.

I shook my head, sighed, and flamed up a blunt. I was just through with this whole situation.

EllaSoul Productions

Chapter 10

Brooke

"One day, you'll ask me what is more important; me, you, or my life. Of course, I'll say, 'my life', and you will walk away not knowing that you are my life" - Unknown

I was shocked, to say the least, when Khan asked me to step outside and talk to him. I know I may come off as a bitch, but I genuinely cared for and loved Khan. He was so sweet and loving behind his thug exterior. Truth is, I'm secretly jealous of Alani. He was so gentle with her and that's how I wanted him to be with me.

As I played the cut and watched how he was with her, I longed for him to be the same way with me. I know I could find another nigga to do the same for me, a man that will love me flaws and all, but I wanted him. From his long dreads to his straight teeth, to his chiseled, tatted up abs to his mannerisms, he was nothing but the truth. Oh, and let's not forget that anaconda that he has dangling between his legs, along with the fact that he knows how to work it.

Khan has the power to make a bitch crawl up the walls while he's dicking her down. When I first saw how big his dick was, I admit I was a little

43

skeptical about fucking him; his dick looked as if he could fuck up a bitch's uterus. But the first time we made love, he showed me that he wasn't just some nigga that ran the city. He made my body reach new heights of pleasure that I didn't even know were possible.

That was the night I fell in love with a dog ass nigga, and I'd been riding that wave ever since. He'd taken me through highs and lows, and even after all the times he told me that he didn't want to be with me, I still felt like we had a fighting chance at a relationship... if only he would take it there with me.

I used to always sit back, ask myself, and wonder, "what Alani could do for him that I couldn't?" Why did she have this hold on him that I couldn't shake him from? Maybe it was time for me to throw in the towel, wave my white flag in surrender, and just let them have their happily ever after. I mean for real, fucking with a nigga like Khan, he was definitely bound to fuck up again, even if it wasn't with me.

"Aye, I just want to holla at you real quick. I'm going to make this shit quick. I'm not even going to stand here and say that the shit I been on with you is a mistake because you don't make mistakes that often; it then becomes a choice. But all that shit wasn't supposed to happen, especially as often as it did. I love my girl, real nigga shit, and

44

that's where I want to be. But I will apologize for giving you any false hope that we would ever be together."

With each word he spoke, he drove another knife through my heart and it took everything in me to remain strong and not shed a tear. I stood there stone-faced, trying to keep my composure while he continued.

"You're a good girl. You just need to wait for the right nigga to come along and treat you the way you're supposed to be treated. Not a nigga like me – I can't even treat my girl right. You see firsthand the shit I put her through fucking around with you. I ain't no good for anybody, but by the grace of God, she still wants be with me. Just keep your head up and the right nigga, naw scratch that, the right MAN gone come along and treat you like somebody… that man just ain't me."

He kissed my cheek and walked back in the house. I just stood there and let silent tears burn down my face. The only man I'd ever loved had broken my heart yet again. Only this time, it felt like it was our last dance. Khan was finally walking out of my life for good and there was nothing that could be done about it.

I had to get out of here and away from him, and I had to do it quick. He was no good for me and I knew it, but that didn't stop the attraction that I had

45

for him or the fact that I loved him more than life itself. I just knew that I needed to step away and take a moment to myself, a moment for Brooke. I walked through the backyard toward the front of the house, got in my car, drove off, and didn't look back.

EllaSoul Productions

Chapter 11

Alani

♫ I'm in love with a thug, I'm in love with a gangster, yeah ♫

Once Khan came back into the house, we were all just sitting around conversing, and drinking like we always did at Mama Megan's house. I don't know where Brooke went, but I really didn't care. It was just a chill moment and it felt good not to have any drama going on for the moment.

Mama Megan came back into the room.

"I hope y'all worked through all that bullshit and everything is solved. I don't want to hear about none of that shit again because then I'm going to be forced to fuck y'all up. Now get the fuck out my house; I got company coming over," she told us dismissively.

"Damn Ma, it's like that? Who you got coming over here that we have to go?" Bam asked, being her regular nosey self. I tell you, Bam and Megan could have been related as crazy as they were.

"None of yo' damn business, now carry y'all asses on!" She yelled at us.

We were still sitting around, ignoring her ass so she reiterated, "Get the fuck out so I can clean my

EllaSoul Productions

house, wash my pussy, and get me some dick. Damn, y'all cock blocking. Y'all must think I'm playing," she yelled walking away.

Knowing Mama Megan, you never knew what she had up her damn sleeve, so we all got the hell out of dodge. The last time, her ass came out naked and the last thing I wanted to see was her fur burger again. I still had nightmares about it to this day.

I decided to go hit up the trap and Khan and Bam followed suit. Regardless of what we were going through, when it came time to getting money, that was our top priority. When we got there, my niggas Rock, Ron, and Mont were all posted up getting money like they were supposed to be.

They were the most loyal niggas on our team and I wouldn't trade those niggas for the world. I nodded to all of them and walked in the house to do count. Usually, it was me, Bam, and Khan, but he lagged behind out front with his niggas, which was fine by me. I wanted to rap with Bam anyway. I know everybody thought I was cocaine crazy for making him go and talk to Brooke, but me being a woman, I knew that she needed closure to actually move the fuck on. I just hoped it didn't come back to bite me in the ass.

Once we got all the bags, counters, and rubber bands out, I started right in.

48

"Aye, real shit sis, I'm sick and tired of Khan's bullshit. He straight lied to a bitch face knowing good and God damn well he fucked that hoe. Man, for real, I looked straight into that bitch's eyes man, and she really in love with his ass. I'm a lot of things but stupid ain't one of them. He was giving that hoe some shit that was only supposed to belong to me and I don't take too kindly to that shit. I'm so sick of him and the shit he come with," I said with my attitude on one hundred but my mind still on the task at hand. I let nothing distract me from my money.

I had a rainy-day fund stashed away that nobody knew about, not even Bam and she's my bottom bitch.

"No disrespect sis, you know I love you and Khan like my real siblings, but are you really tired of him?" Bam asked me with a questioning glare.

"Yeah, bitch! Ain't that what the fuck I just said?" I snapped back, defensively.

"I said 'no disrespect', so watch your tone. I'm not your fucking enemy, nor am I the one who fucked your man. As I was saying, he fucks with countless bitches day in and day out to the point when people don't even feel the need to tell you because you ain't gone leave his dog ass. Now don't get me wrong, I'm not denying his love for you, but like my girl K. Michelle said, 'you can't raise a

49

man', and he still got some growing up to do. Every time he fucks up, you take his ass right back like he ain't done shit. Why would he act right if he can have his cake and eat it, too? You know what they say, 'why buy the cow when you can get the milk for free'."

As I sat there, I thought about what she was saying. Everything she said was true and that's what was pissing me off. Was I really sitting around looking like a weak bitch in front of everybody? Was everybody laughing at me for staying with a man that's holding court with a plethora of buzzard bitches? The amount of questions running through my head was driving me crazy.

My head started to spin and I felt faint. Whoever said that being in love is a great thing lied. Well, not completely, but the feeling of having a broken heart will make you feel as though you're sick. The craziest part about it is I still had a man and we're technically still together, but Khan might as well have left me high and dry with the ache that I was feeling in my chest behind his actions.

Then, Bam continued. "I mean, Khan is the only nigga you've ever been with. Maybe it's time you get out there, test the waters a little bit and see what's out there. Now, I'm not saying turn into a little thot, nor am I trying to tell you what to do, but just think about what it is that you want out of your relationship with him."

EllaSoul Productions

Just as we finished our conversation, we wrapped up the last of the money and threw it in duffle bags. I was about to shoot Khan a text when he bopped his ass into the room.

"Y'all done already?" He questioned with a surprised look on his face.

"Yeah, nigga. You know we never lacking," Bam told him matter-of-factly.

"So, y'all couldn't wait for me?" he asked seriously.

I was about to clown his ass, but instead I countered with, "time waits for no man."

I walked out the room with Bam in tow, leaving him to do drop-offs. Fuck it, he could take Rock with him. I had a lot to think about, so I had Bam drop me off at my mother's house. My car was there, in addition to the fact that I was still blown about the whole Brooke situation. I didn't want to sleep next to the lying ass nigga I called my man.

So much for a monogamous relationship, I thought.

Chapter 12

Khan

♫ I know I swore that I'd never break your heart no more ♫

I know I really fucked up, but damn, my shawty had never given me the cold shoulder like that. I knew I needed to get my shit together but those hoes just kept calling me. Don't get me wrong, my girl's a bad bitch and she satisfied me, but for some reason I couldn't seem turn these hoes down; they threw the ass at me and I caught it, simple as that.

I don't understand females, man. I can be out with my niggas and a bitch will try to holla' at me. Then I tell her I got a wife at home only for her to still try her hand at cuffing the kid. Like, what part of the game is that? Even if I'm with my girl out to dinner or some shit, hoes will still fuck with me. They'll slide me their number when La'La isn't paying attention or if she steps away to go to the ladies' room.

I'd never understand how females operate, but at the same time, I'm still a young nigga on the come up. Bitches see a nigga with a lil' money in his pockets and they're ready to propose to a nigga. I could throw a bitch a few hundred dollars and she'd be on her knees, blessing the throne less than five minutes later. When you have money, power, respect, and an abundance of pussy being thrown at you daily, you're not thinking about the good girl that's down for you that you have at home.

I grabbed two of the duffle bags that Alani and Bam packed up then called for Rock to come and get the other two. I wanted to get this shit over with so that I could get home to my baby. I knew that she wasn't feeling me right now, but that ain't nothing some good dick can't cure. Once I put this long and strong on her, she'd be loving on me again, acting as if nothing had ever happened.

Bitches can pump fake like dick doesn't solves problems, but it definitely does. I long stroke a bitch into submission to the point where she sleeps like a baby and no longer cared about what the fuck it was she was so-called "mad" at. I'm far from a cocky nigga, I just know what I'm capable of and what I have.

From the outside looking in, it might seem like I don't give a fuck about La'La, but I do. That girl means the world to me and I want to spend forever and a day with her. If I gotta spend the next hundred years showing her, then so be it. My baby is literally in a class all her own, she was so fly effortlessly. I'd yet to meet a bitch that was on her level and I didn't think that I ever would. She's five-foot-three with a pecan tan complexion and hair that hangs just past her shoulders when curly and a little longer when straight. She has hips and ass for days,

53

with average C-cup breasts… but they're perfect for me. All I need is a handful. Her cheek bones were well-defined, and she stayed on point.

I wouldn't trade her for the world, but for some reason, I just couldn't seem to get my shit together. I'm a boss ass nigga that runs the city with my hands in a little bit of everything. When bitches see a fly, young, boss ass nigga like me, they see a meal ticket. They don't even want me for real, they just like the idea of being with a nigga like me and what I come with.

After Rock and I made the drops, I took him back to the trap he ran and made my way home. When I got to the five-bedroom, four bath townhouse that I shared with Alani, all the lights were out. I knew she was most likely sleep already so I used one of the guestrooms to shower so that I wouldn't wake her.

When I walked into our bedroom, I was shocked to see that the bed was completely made. One thing about Alani and I was that we never went to sleep mad at each other. We always literally kissed and made up, and maybe fucked. But this time, I knew it wasn't going to be that easy. I wholeheartedly believed in the saying, "happy wife, happy life", and I'd fucked up royally this time.

I decided to text her to see where her head was at.

EllaSoul Productions

Me: Bae, where you at?

Wifey: Where I'm wanted

Me: And where is that?

Wifey: I'm where I'm at and you're where you at. See you when I see ya. (Laughing Emoji)

Me: La'La I'm not playing with your dumb ass, bring your ass home! You're a married fucking woman!

Wifey: (Looks down at bare ring finger) If you liked it then you should have put a ring on it (in my Beyoncé voice)

I didn't even text back. She could be so childish and stubborn at times. To be completely honest, when we first started fucking with each other, it was a trivial bet between and my niggas on who could bag the most bitches. Of course, I won, but even if I didn't, I still won the best prize of all: Alani.

Out of all the girls, Alani stood out. She had an aura about her that just made you want to be in her space. Throughout all the hoes, lies, and everything, she'd stuck around. Her beauty, mindset, personality, and character prevailed the rest. She had proven her loyalty to me time and time again, now it was time for me to return the favor. I had to get back in my baby's good graces and I had the perfect plan.

Chapter 13

Alani

♫ Longing for my baby to love me more ♫

I answered my phone for a screaming Bam.

"Let's go bitch, I got a whole day planned for us!" She screamed into the phone.

Today was my birthday but I wanted nothing more than to lay in bed. It'd been a week and I still hadn't taken my ass home yet. I'd been staying between my mama's and Bam's houses, considering that I had a room at both. I still hadn't built up the gumption to take my ass home and sleep in the same bed as a nothing ass nigga.

My mama always taught me that if you lie down with dogs then you'll get up with fleas. Sometimes, love wasn't enough to keep a relationship going. No relationship is perfect, but the perfection comes from two people working on their problems and aren't willing to give up. Khan wasn't working on any of the problems that we had, even though he was the problem.

I looked too good to stay with a nigga that couldn't do right by me. I'm a damn good catch, so any nigga that fucks me over is a fool. They say one man's trash is another man's treasure, but I believe that one man's treasure is still another man's treasure, and I'm definitely a muhfuckin' treasure. Men will get the girl that everybody wants only to forget that she is still the girl that everybody wants.

I chose to stay at my mom's house last night, knowing that Bam was going to try and get me to do something today. To say that I wasn't in the mood to do anything would be an understatement.

"I don't feel like it, Bam" I groaned into the phone.

"Okay, you got it" she stated nonchalantly before hanging up. I was surprised, but grateful that she didn't put up a fight in attempts to get me out of the house.

Even though it was one o'clock in the afternoon, I was still in bed chilling. Happy that I got her off my case with little to no effort, I rolled over in bed. My mother made me breakfast and brought it up to me, so I had no reason to get up. She understood that I was going through some things, so she didn't pressure me to get up and do anything. I cut on the Pandora app on my phone and plugged in my headphones. I was vibin' to Erykah Badu radio when I suddenly burst into tears. They were playing our song and all I could think about was him.

I threw my head under the comforter and cried my heart out. It felt as if my soul was bleeding. Khan was my addiction and I was currently going through withdrawals without him. Love wasn't supposed to hurt like this and I felt as if nothing could ease my sorrow.

It's the worst when the only person that could ease your pain is the same person who is cause of it. I loved Khan more than life itself, but I couldn't, for the life of me, understand why he couldn't just do right by me. Did I not fuck him good enough? I was dying to know why he couldn't keep his shit in his pants.

If a man chose to cheat, not that it's right one way or the other, he should have his hoes so in line that his ole lady/wife don't know shit about them. Those bitches should never pick up the phone to call another man's ole lady, let alone have her number. A side hoe, or mistress for that matter, should never feel comfortable enough to address the wife.

My sulking was short-lived because I was doused with ice cold water. I snatched the covers off my head and there was Bam with a big ass pot of water.

"What the fuck, Sophie?" I screamed, calling her by her government name.

"Get the fuck up because there's more where that came from," she said picking up another pot.

58

The no nonsense look she gave me told me she wasn't going to give up.

"Alright, bitch. Damn," I gave in, getting up, not that I wanted to continue sleeping in a soaking wet bed anyway. I walked over to my closet to find something to wear.

"Don't worry about getting cute just throw this on," she said throwing me a pair of yoga pants and tank top.

"Sure thing mother dearest," I replied sarcastically. Why couldn't everybody just let me be sappy in peace?

I wanted to cry about my lost love and failed relationship, not smile in a bunch of people's faces. Birthdays stopped meaning anything to me a long time ago. I no longer cared to celebrate a day that only marked me getting closer to my death.

After getting my hygiene in order, we were out the door. We hopped inside Bam's black-on-black five series Benz and peeled out.

"Where the fuck we going?" I asked her after driving around for about five minutes. I was beyond irritated that she'd just basically dragged me out of the house.

"Shut the fuck up, sit back, and ride. I'm so sick of the shit yo' ass been on this past week. You

EllaSoul Productions

need to suck that sappy ass shit up. You supposed to be a grown ass woman, so act like it. When I told you that you might need a break, I didn't mean ignore his ass for a fucking week. Your dumb ass should've told him what was up first. Plus, by you ignoring him, you've been slacking on the business tip. You're never supposed to let a nigga get you off your square," Bam said, chewing me a new asshole.

"But I…" that was all I got out before she cut me off.

"Shut up, I'm talking now. You keep playing these childish ass games and you're going to end up alone. You're my bitch and I love your ugly ass to the death of me, but you got some soul searching to do. You're never supposed to lose yourself in a man, because when he gone you don't have shit. Now, we are about to go get these massages done so we can turn up tonight. After all, you only have one birthday a year."

Bam sure knew how to shut my ass up. It was then that I noticed we'd stopped in front of Heavenly Touch, an upscale salon in the heart of Norfolk. Heavenly Touch was owned by my girl, Diamond, and she was a beast at it all. Her salon specialized in everything. As soon as we walked in the door, we were greeted by her staff with a glass of Dom.

"Welcome Mrs. Thomas and Miss Young, I'm Erica and this is Tay. Y'all will be getting the works today courtesy of Mr. Thomas, follow me right this way."

The vibe of the girl who had introduced herself as Erica was off. I didn't like the way she looked at me. I know I'm a lil' baddie and a heavy-duty cutie, but the jealousy that she held in her eyes didn't settle with me. She looked like she didn't like me even though I'd never seen her ass before.

We walked into a room that was dimly lit with dozens of candles omitting the sweet scents of lavender and vanilla, which just so happens to be mine and Bam's favorites.

"You ladies can strip down to your birthday suits and put on theses robes we've provided here for you," Erica said then turned to walk out the room.

"Oh yeah, here you go Mrs. Thomas." she added handing me an envelope. "It's from your husband." And with that she left the room.

I wanted to tell them that my name wasn't Thomas, it was Clark, and that I wasn't married, but decided against it. I opened the envelope and it was a poem from Khan. We always wrote little poems to each other; it was cheesy, but we always looked forward to them from each other. This poem was entitled, *Your Helping Hand*.

61

Good fortune brought me to your door

And when your heard me knock

I was invited in without the turning of a lock

Your welcome was as warm as if you had expected me

And just as if your heart had longed to have my company

You wore a smile of love and you made me feel at ease

And in so many other ways,

You did your best to please me

And when I saw your kindly eyes

And touched your helping hand

I knew I could go to you,

However late in the night

And you'd be at my side

Until the morning light

"Aww," I said out loud, but more to him even though he wasn't here physically. He knew that his poems could always bring a smile to my face.

"Let me see," Bam said, snatching it out of my hand. After she finished reading it, she threw it back at me.

"Eww y'all too cute for me."

"Shut up bitch – you just peanut butter and jealous," I shot back sticking out my tongue.

We continued to get undressed and made small talk while we waited for our masseuses to come back.

"You ready ladies?" Erica's extra salty ass came back and asked.

"Yes, we're ready," I replied, following her. I got a funny vibe from her but chose to ignore it, for now.

We got deep tissue massages, facials, our hair done, and our faces beat to the fucking gawds. Diamond was the only one I would allow to touch my hair, so I didn't care how long I had to wait because she was always worth it. I walked out of there feeling like new money. My twenty-two-inch Malaysian deep body wave had me feeling myself, not that I didn't have a reason to. Now I just needed my attire to look the part as well. We must've been in there for a minute, because the sun was setting when we were leaving.

While I was laying around sulking over Khan this past week, I'd been neglecting to take care of myself. Diamond cracked many jokes about the bird's nest that rested at the top of my sew-in.

When we got in the car, I turned to Bam.

"Thank you, sis. I really needed that."

"Don't thank me, bitch. You need to thank your man who you have been treating like shit, might I add. He really loves you girl, and don't think that I'm trying to downplay the fact that he fucks up from time to time. But he really is a good dude under that fuck nigga exterior."

"I know, sis. But sometimes I wonder if it all worth it. Like really, how much can one heart take?" I said solemnly, thinking about all the shit he'd put me through.

"Perk up, hoe it's yo' day and tonight is about to be lit," Bam yelled, sensing my change in demeanor.

I cracked a small smile while giving Bam the side eye, wondering what she and Khan had up their sleeves. But for now, I was going to sit back and enjoy the benefits of it all.

Whatever he had planned better be good. I damn sure deserved it after all he'd done.

EllaSoul Productions

He'd better go hard or go home. Material things didn't make or break me, nor was it the reason I was with him, but it did help ease the blows that he delivered to my heart time and time again.

EllaSoul Productions

Chapter 14

Alani

I leaned back in my seat and closed my eyes, sinking into the leather. Then, Bam turned on our fucking anthem, *Candy Lady* by Gucci Mane and 1017 Brick Squad. We were turning up in the car, singing along to all the words. After our song went off, Bam handed me another envelope identical to the one the masseuse gave me.

"What's this?" I asked her.

"It's a lottery ticket. What you think, hoe? Just open it," her obnoxious ass yelled.

Instead of responding, I just opened the envelope and saw that it was another poem titled *Never Say Goodbye*.

Never say "Goodbye"

But "See you later"

A departure or farewell

That ensures that we will cross paths again

I will always be here for you

So there is no need to speak in such a manner

I'll never leave you, but I might be momentarily gone away

But I promise to be right back

So promise me you'll do the same

And let our love fly and never say goodbye

And let our love die

You're my yesterday and my yesteryears

My today and all my tomorrows

*And hoping and wanting that I could be yours
again*

So why say goodbye?

I promise without your love I'm sure to die

So just say, "see you later" but

Never Say "Goodbye"

By the end, I was in tears. Here I was, ready to leave the only man I'd ever been with, knowing deep down that with him was where I wanted to be.

"Stop fucking crying bitch before you fuck up your face. Let's go," Bam snapped when we got to her house.

When we got inside, I walked straight to my room. As soon as I flipped on the light, my eyes fell on a garment bag that was laid across the bed, along with three jewelry boxes, and a shoe box.

EllaSoul Productions

I opened the garment bag first and there laid a beautiful, black and white fitted Christian Dior Houndstooth Tweed Hi-Lo dress. I then opened the shoe box that held a pair of black and white Giuseppe Zanotti embellished suede stilettos. This man was really pulling out all the stops, trying to lay it on extra thick. The contents of the jewelry boxes made my damn heart stop. He'd bought me a presidential Rolex, a pair of diamond studs, and a diamond necklace. I was already going to be looking good, but now I was about to be shutting shit down.

He knew he couldn't buy his way back into my heart, but this was a damn good start, no bullshit. I stripped out of my clothes so that I could shower, right before Bam bust in the damn room like Rambo.

"Bitch what he get you?" She asked me.

I moved out of the way so that she could see the contents of the bed and she screamed.

"Ohh bitch, we gone be killing the game tonight."

I'm a nudist by nature so she'd seen me in the buff more times than I cared to count. I followed her to bedroom so that I could see what she was wearing. Khan had copped her something too, so she was going to be wearing an outfit just as fly as mine, but it was a little simpler. It was cute nonetheless, just not as sexy as mine.

68

"Alright hoe, we got somewhere to be by eleven, so get that ass in the shower," she said smacking my ass.

"I was about to until I was so rudely interrupted," I countered with a playful side eye.

"Whatever just be ready," she replied and walked away.

I hopped into my shower and lathered my body with my Country Chic body wash from Bath and Body Works. I was careful not to fuck up my hair and makeup, so I threw on a satin shower cap.

As I was washing, my mind quickly shifted back to Khan. I knew I could forgive him, but could he start being true to me and be the man that I needed? I knew that we were still young and shit, but if he needed some time to get some things out of his system then that's what the fuck his ass needed to say. I honestly didn't know how much more I could take from him. He literally only had one more time to fuck up with me and it'd be curtains for that ass. I must've been away with my thoughts because the water had turned cold on me. I hastily washed once more and got out.

I dried off and moisturized my entire body with raw shea butter. I got dressed, put on my Rolex and earrings, and walked to Bam's room so she could put on my necklace for me.

"Oh, kill em! Oh, kill em," Bam exclaimed excitedly.

I zipped up her dress, then handed her my necklace and turned around for her to put it on my neck and zip me up.

We still had time to kill, so we popped the top on some red berry Cîroc and cut on some music. I stood up, swaying from side to side with my glass in my hand, just vibing.

"Damn boo, that ass is poking out."

Bam smacked my ass, so I started twerking on her. I knew my body was like that so there was no shame in my game. I loved the fact that I could always be me uninhibited with her and it was times like this that made me love her even more. She's just so uncouth and unfiltered, but I love it. I wouldn't trade my bitch for the world. Plus, she's as thorough as they come and loyal as fuck.

In the past, we'd attempted to let other people in our circle and it had always ended with either me or Bam, or sometimes both of us, beating their asses. Ever since then, we've always kept our circle small. Besides doing business with people, it's just me and my Sophie.

After playing around for a while and getting a little buzzed, we grabbed our clutches and walked towards the door. It was eleven thirty when we left the house on our way to the Chic Lounge, run by this girl named Envy that Bam and I went to school with. It's an upscale bar and lounge that catered to a more sophisticated crowd. It was one of the few places that you could chill and hang out without having to really worry about fights or shooting. Envy was really cool, but I didn't fuck with many bitches outside of Bam. We'd all chilled a few times when her husband Adonis did business with Khan and Rock.

When Bam and I pulled up, we hopped out the car like ghetto royalty, tossed $100 and the keys to the valet, and proceeded inside. With each click of my heels, my anxiety increased, but I kept a stone look on my face; I looked too damn good was what I told myself. Plus, drinking damn near a whole bottle with Bam before we left the house, and the blunt we smoked on the way here, had calmed my racing heart. I couldn't help but wonder what he had in store for me on the other side of this door. My baby had got the red carpet rolled out for me and everything. Everyone knew our faces, so we just walked right in. The bouncer must've told them that we'd arrived because as soon as I stepped in, the spotlight shinned directly on me.

Envy was up on the stage at the microphone.

"The guest of honor has arrived. I would like to give a special "happy birthday" to my girl, La'La. Live it up boo, It's your day!" She said smiling while everybody that came out clapped for me. I hated being in the limelight. I preferred to play the cut, but I put on a smile… for the moment. Not only that, but I'm low-key shy.

Envy stepped back and Khan walked up on the stage looking like he had just stepped out of a GQ magazine, rocking a suit that matched my dress down to a tee.

"Alright y'all mother fuckers settle down. Thank you all for coming out to help me bring my baby's birthday in right. She deserves the world and then some. I love you, Princess."

I couldn't help but smile. He was so sexy, and I could see the sincerity in his eyes. He had his dreads pulled back and the cluster diamonds in his ears that matched his grill were damn near blinding the crowd.

I mouthed the words, "Thank you" to him with my cheeks burning from blushing so hard.

"Baby girl come here," he said gesturing for me to come closer.

I looked around and noticed that Bam was gone already, so I made my way toward the front of the stage. I made a mental note to get her ass when I saw her again. When I made it to the front, the lights dimmed.

"Baby this is for you. I love you, girl," Khan said and then the music started playing.

All I wanna do

Is keep it light (keep it light)

Keep you satisfied

All I wanna do (is make it right make it right)

Make you smile tonight

All I wanna do is give you that thing, play you that song you and your girlfriends sing

All I wanna do is get you back tonight

I was in pain from laughing so fucking hard. If you wonder why I was laughing it's because my baby can't sing a fucking lick and he was trying his hardest to sing a rendition of Robin Thicke's song, *Get Her Back*. This nigga even had Envy in here singing back up for his ass.

He was up on that damn stage preforming and making me fall in love all over again. When the song was over, I was in tears and clutching my stomach from laughing so hard. The whole crowd was laughing like they were in a fucking comedy show.

Khan grabbed my hand to help me on the small stage and put his arm around my waist.

73

"Alright y'all can stop laughing at me now," he said laughing himself.

He then turned to me on a more serious note.

"Baby girl, you're the only person in the world that I would make a fool of myself over. I love you more than life and I'll spend the rest of my days showing you just that. You make me want to be a better man and you're the only one that I want to bare my kids and carry my last name. If you give a chance to right all my wrongs, I'll promise to make it worth your while. I guess I'm saying all this to say, 'will you marry me Alani and become my Mrs. Thomas?'" he said getting on one knee.

How could I say "no" after his rendition of Robin Thicke and him holding out a ring that rivaled the size of NeNe Leakes'?

"Hell yeah I will," I screamed, jumping into his arms right after he slid the ring on my finger.

"I got one more thing for my future wife then I'mma let y'all go ahead and enjoy your night." After he addressed the crowd, he pulled out and envelope similar to the ones from earlier. "Now this one is titled *My Bitch*.

You ask why I call you "My Bitch" my bitch

It's 'cause my bitch comes fully equipped

With a fat ass and some big tits

Whatever my bitch wants she can damn well get

She'll have a nigga locked in just from licking her lips

Then jerking off from her moving her hips

My bitch a have niggas gone just from rubbing the dick

Quick fast and in a hurry you'd be throwing her bricks

Then she turns around and sell you back all yo' shit

But she never gives up that clit because she knows that clit is my shit

Now tell me why I can't call that bitch "My Bitch"."

After he concluded his poem, he kissed me and we walked off the stage hand in hand. *Now that's how you get your bitch back*, I laughed thinking to myself.

Chapter 15

Khan

♫ Baby don't turn the page I read the story it ends with you and me ♫

My squad and I were just chilling in the VIP section. It felt great to have my baby sitting on my lap and back in my arms. I loved the feeling and didn't want to lose it ever again. Alani was in her zone, sipping her Cîroc and twerking that fat ass of hers on my dick.

My shit was all bricked up and I knew she could feel it 'cause she threw her drink back and started making that thang clap in my face and shit. I stood up and started grinding on her ass. They were playing one of my favorite reggae songs, *Boom Bye Bye* by Buju Banton. I might not be able to sing, but I could dance a little bit. It didn't help that I had some Henn Dog in my system.

"Damn get a fucking room, don't nobody wanna see all that shit," Bam's uncouth ass yelled like she wasn't over there shaking her ass on Rock.

I wondered when they started fucking around, but that shit wasn't any of my business, so I ain't even bother to say shit about it.

I'd had enough of this dry humping shit. I grabbed my shawty hand and took her to the bathroom. I checked to make sure all the stalls were empty then locked the door.

"What are you doing Khan? You can't wait until we get home?" She asked me like she didn't already know what time it was.

"Fuck no, now bend that juicy ass over," I growled.

She obliged by hiking her dress and tooting that ass in the air. She had the nerve to act like she didn't want it but her pussy wouldn't be as wet as it was if she didn't.

My shorty loved fucking me just as much as I loved fucking her. I knew I'd created a fucking monster. La'La could cum just from shooting somebody or counting money. I smiled at the woman in my life and the person she'd become.

She didn't have on any panties, just like I liked it. With the sweet smell her pussy was releasing, my dick was just gone have to wait because I stuck my face right in it.

"Oh shit bae, slow down," Alani whimpered out but I ain't give a fuck. I missed the shit out of her ass and wanted to show Miss Kitty I missed her just as much.

I was devouring Miss Kitty and knew she missed me just as much when she squirted all in my face. Alani tried to move, but I grabbed her and held on tight. I could feel her legs about to give out on her when she creamed again.

"Bae I can't take it," she cried out.

"Yes, you can," I countered and tried to shut her up by plunging this Louisville slugger up in her guts.

"Oh, fuck daddy," she screamed out so loud the whole club could probably hear her, even over the music.

I picked up one if her legs and held it in the crook of my arm. It was bliss inside her walls and thinking about me being the only one to enter her had a nigga floating. I was beating Alani's box up, trying to write my name on her shit. She had reached under her and was rubbing her clit.

"Yeah bae, play with that shit just like that."

I had to slow down to keep from exploding prematurely.

She was so wet her juices had soaked the floor, and I had to fight to keep my footing to from slipping and busting my ass.

"Bae I'm about to cum. Cum with me," La'La cried hoarsely.

"I'm right behind you baby girl," I told her right before I bust so hard I know my baby had to be knocked up with at least triplets.

"Damn baby, you must have really missed me," she said, commenting on our sex session holding a hand full of paper towels to clean me off.

"You know we both did," I said pointing at my dick.

"Boy you crazy. Let's go before Bam bust up in this bitch," she said laughing but I didn't find shit funny. Bam would come up in this bitch blasting if she thought something was wrong with La'La. That was one person's bad side that I did not want to be on. Bam had a couple loose screws, but one thing that could never be denied was Bam's loyalty.

We made our way back to VIP and sat down as if nothing happened.

"Bout time y'all found your ways back. I was about to fuck some shit up!" Bam scolded us.

We just locked eyes and shared a laugh. We knew her ass too damn well.

"What the fuck is so damn funny? I wanna laugh too," Bam asked seriously.

"Nothing sis, you just sit your little fire cracker ass down over there," I told her.

"Mmhmm, whatever," she said rolling her eyes.

Words couldn't explain the feeling I had that my girl forgave and agreed to marry me. If pulling this stunt didn't get her to come back to the kid, I didn't know what would. I usually didn't give up on something I wanted as bad as I want La'La, but if she didn't take a nigga back, I was about to throw in the towel. I figured our time had just expired, but accepting my proposal told a nigga she loved me just as much, if not more than I loved her.

For the rest of the night, we turned up and enjoyed ourselves. Adonis and Envy joined us in the VIP section. Life was good, but I couldn't knock the feeling of some bullshit brewing in the cosmos. Whatever it was, I just hoped I was ready for it.

EllaSoul Productions

Chapter 16

Alani

8 months later

♫ When I look into your eyes I see real love ♫

Life had been great for me and my whole family. Business was booming and I didn't have any complaints. Bam and Rock finally moved in together as if everybody didn't already know they were creeping around, I was eight months pregnant, and Bam was right behind me at six months. What the fuck were the odds of us being knocked up at the same time? I know I got knocked up around my birthday, it was that dope dick Khan gave me in the bathroom at my party. But for some reason, I felt as if this was only the calm before the storm.

If somebody was feeling the need to come for my family, then they're in for a rude awakening. We're all a force to be reckoned with. So whatever it was, I just hoped they were locked and loaded, for their sake, that is.

I was in the midst of planning my wedding, as I had been for the last several months, because I wanted to be Mrs. Thomas before I pushed my baby into this world. I'd just left the doctor's office and I couldn't be happier that my bundle of joy was healthy. Neither I nor Khan wanted to know what we were having until he or she popped out.

I wanted to be surprised while in the labor and delivery room. Having a child was the greatest gift God could give someone, especially when they were made out of love. Each flutter in my stomach made my soul smile. Making the decision to have a baby was momentous. It was to decide forever to have your heart walking around outside of your body.

I was already in love with my baby and they were not even here yet.

My baby shower was next week and it's just going to be a small gathering at my mother-in-law's house. I just told everybody to buy unisex colors for everything, and Khan had already bought everything that our baby would need and then some.

We are going to wait until the baby was born to buy them the things I wanted to be gender specific. I wanted to be prepared for my first child, but I also didn't want to ruin it by knowing what it was. We had more money than we knew what to do with, so money was not an object.

*****

The day of my baby shower was here and I was ecstatic. I had on an all-white Chanel maxi dress, and my stomach looked huge. Khan always made it his business to let me know that I looked

82

fine, but whenever I stepped in front of that full-length mirror, all I saw was a fat ass beached whale.

"Princess, you ready?" Khan yelled to me up the stairs.

"Yes baby, I'm coming now," I replied while making my way down the stairs.

"Baby I can't find my new Birkin bag that I bought to match this dress, my keys, or my phone?" I whined.

The great thing about me being pregnant was I had no morning sickness or any of that shit. The only thing I had were cravings for weird foods; I'm always hungry, and I've turned into the biggest brat in the world. Well, at least that's what everybody else says, but I just want what I want when I want it. If they'd just let me have my way I'd be good.

"It's right here girl, now bring that ass on here. How you gone be late to your own baby shower?"

I rolled my eyes at him, "Well at least I'll be fashionably late."

"Looking at me like that is going to make us even later because I'm ready to bend your sexy ass over that chair and rearrange your organs," he said eyeing me lustfully.

EllaSoul Productions

"Khan, that sounds like it'll hurt. So not sexy," I laughed.

"Whatever you say mama, but the way you eyed the kid's dick print lets me know you want me to break you off, so bend that ass over," Khan demanded.

I hated that he knew me like the back of his hand. This baby had me horny all the time.

"Whatever you say, daddy," I purred and hiked up my dress. I didn't have on any panties because it is just more comfortable like that.

"Naw, lay back onto the couch first."

I don't care what anybody says, Khan might just love eating my pussy just as much as I loved getting it eaten – shit, maybe more. Khan dove in and I grinded my pussy in his face. Like Nicki Minaj said, I was tryna put this pussy on his side burns. He didn't mind, though. After bringing me to an orgasm, he flipped me over so that I was on all fours but was careful not to harm the baby.

Khan slid up in me with ease and precision and started off stroking me slow. I needed this nut like yesterday, so I started throwing my ass back into him. Not wanting me to outdo him, he grabbed hips and started going for broke on my shit.

Khan is all man, so it's just in his nature to dominate during sex. Fuck making love, I lived for that rough sex and he knew it. Khan grabbed my sew-in, wrapped it around his hand, and pulled my hair slightly. That didn't do shit but make my pussy wetter.

"Right there, daddy!" I screamed and he obliged.

"That's right baby girl wet my shit up" Khan grunted.

I felt an orgasm building up and I couldn't contain it.

"Baby, I'm coming," I moaned.

"What you telling me for? Let that shit out girl," Khan said, slapping my ass.

I came so hard it was like my soul left my fucking body.

"Argh!" I grunted and Khan came shortly after me.

I rolled over and collapsed on the couch. Khan grabbed a rag to clean me up. I usually would have hopped back into the shower, but I was tired and already running behind, so a hoe bath would just have to do for now. We both got cleaned up, straightened out our clothes, and were out the door.

When we got to Mama Megan's house, it was packed.

So much for a small gathering, I thought.

I walked around and mingled for a little bit. I put a fake smile on for all the congratulations from a whole slew of people that I didn't even know. I just wanted to get to the kitchen and eat. My baby smelled all that good food before I did, and I knew Megan's ass threw down in the kitchen. The slight kicks to my stomach let me know that my baby was as hungry as I was.

The first chance I got, I was in there filling my plate up. She had it set up like a buffet in this mug and I wanted a little bit of everything. I walked out the kitchen with the biggest cup I could find filled with Kool-Aid, a plate fit for a king, and a smile plastered on my face.

"Hey fat ass," I heard a voice say, when I was ducked off in the corner stuffing my face.

I stopped my eating and looked up into the face of Shaunda. She was a bitch that I'd gone to school with back in the day, and Bam and I hung out with her from time to time. But, she was one of those hoes that you had to feed with a long-handled spoon. I kept that bitch on a short leash because she was too shady for my taste. It didn't help that I felt like she wanted my nigga. I didn't have any proof, but I didn't feel like I needed any. A hunch was

86

enough for me to cut that bitch off. What the fuck do I look like sitting around waiting for a bitch to push up on my nigga?

"What's up," I said and continued eating my food. She knew I didn't fuck with her like that so why she was even here was beyond me. Even better, who invited her ditzy ass?

"You think you got enough food on that plate? You already look like you're about to pop."

My neck snapped in her direction and I was just about to spaz out on her ass. Instead, I put my plate down, threw my cup of Kool-Aid in her face, and hit her with a quick two-piece. She fell instantly. I knew that bitch was all bark and no bite. That hoe had the nerve to be laying down like she was outlined in chalk. She used to always talk shit and then have me and Bam wrecking for her. She couldn't bust a fucking grape in a damn fruit fight.

I sat back down, picked up my plate, and continued eating unbothered. I hated when a bean pole looking ass bitch wanna tried to come for somebody. I'm a beautiful and bodacious size fourteen, and even before I was pregnant I was a size twelve, and not one bit ashamed. I loved every bend and curve. Skinny bitches like Shaunda couldn't hold a candle to a bitch like me. I wasn't a sloppy girl and I carried myself well. Any fool can

87

drive straight, but it takes a real man to be able to maneuver down a winding road.

Skinny hoes are always mad at a thick chick for no reason. But for what, though? I wasn't taking any food out of their mouths, so tell me, why they are really mad? Was it because I'm fucking, sucking, and riding the dick of the man they wanted? I couldn't figure it out and I didn't think I wanted to.

Bam rushed over to me.

"Why this bitch on the floor?"

I just shrugged my shoulders like I didn't know shit. Bam kicked her

"Get the fuck up and carry yo' ass on somewhere. You ain't wanted here bitch."

She must've been playing dead or some shit at first because she jumped up and ran outside after hearing Bam.

"I know she said something that bitch always sneak dissing," Bam said, hitting the nail on the head and taking a seat beside me.

I don't even know how she knew something was wrong with me to even come and check on me. But we're so in sync, we always knew when some shit was up with the other.

"Did you get her good, though?" Bam asked.

"You know it bitch," I said, high fiving her. Then, we shared a laugh.

Khan and Rock came rushing in the house over to where we were sitting.

"What the fuck y'all in here fighting for like y'all ain't pregnant as hell?"

"Well tell that bitch to watch her fucking mouth before I punch her in it again," I told him.

"Man, I don't know what the fuck I'mma do with y'all asses," Khan said, walking off. I guess he knew that he couldn't do shit about it.

Pregnant or not, fuck I look like letting a bitch talk out the side of her neck to me? For as long as I could remember, I'd never let a bitch talk to me greasy without making her answer to these hands or these hollow tips.

After I was good and stuffed, we played a few baby shower games, but I was getting tired and still had to stop by the traps before I headed home. Khan would flip if he knew I still was riding through on the regular, especially without him. Rock, on the other hand, knew he couldn't do shit with Bam, so he just ain't say shit about it. I'd been grateful for him not ratting me out to Khan, being that that's his right hand.

89

I found Khan and told him Bam was gone take me home. He told me he was going to chill for a bit, help his mama clean up, stop by the traps, and head home. I figured if he was doing all that, it would give me time to get there first and shit. I knew he would be mad at me when he found out that I did pick-ups and drop-offs, but he'd get over it.

For the most part, I tried to stay home and play the good girlfriend, or should I say, fiancée role, but I missed going out and getting my hands dirty. Bam and I did count and dropped off the work. After all that shit was done, she dropped me off home. I found it weird that Khan wasn't home and I hadn't ran into him at any of the traps, so I shot him a text.

Me: *Where you at?*

Hubby: *At the main trap on the Blvd be home soon. I love you*

Me: *I love you too*

He has been doing well since we got engaged, but now I wasn't so sure. We'd just left the main trap, so we should've run into him… then again, maybe not. I'm at least willing to give him the benefit of the doubt. For now, I was going take a shower and go to bed until I had concrete evidence to believe otherwise.

Chapter 17

Bam

♫ You say I'm crazyyyy! ♫

"I'm so fucking sick of being knocked up. I swear I'm never getting pregnant again," I stressed to La'La while me, her, and Envy were at the last fitting for our dresses for her wedding.

We kept blowing up, so they had to keep altering our dresses, so it was a good thing the wedding was this weekend. Plus, if this bitch poked me one more time, I was fucking her up.

"Girl, you know I am actually happy low-key, but I'm just ready for this little boy to come the fuck out. He's killing me from the inside out. Shit, Rock came home last night, and I was having Braxton Hicks, like real bad, and he was just standing there looking at me all lost in the face and scared. So, I got mad and tried to shoot his ass, but I missed and just grazed his ear."

"What the fuck, Bam? He didn't even do anything," Alani shrieked.

"Exactly my fucking point! He should've been trying to ease some the pain this little boy putting me through. After all, he's the one that has put me into this predicament," I stated matter-of-factly.

I didn't give a damn. He knew what type of bitch I was before he started fucking with me. Now we're bonded for life through the life that was growing inside of me.

"Bitch poke me again and I'll guarantee that your ass will come up missing," I sneered.

She just looked at me and walked away.

"Sophie, stop being mean, and don't be doing that to him. Rock is a good guy," La'La said and Envy cosigned.

"Girl, please. I'll be a little nicer once I drop this load, but until then, he is going to have to live with the bitch I've become," I said, shrugging my shoulders.

"Shit, I was sick one morning last week and he was still sleep and not up to help me, so I cut a couple of his dreads off, then left the scissors and the dreads on the pillow beside his head so he could see the shit when he got up. After that, I got dressed and went to Diamond's to get my hair laid."

"What the fuck, Bam! Rock is too nice for you to be doing him like that. He's such a good guy despite what we do. You shouldn't be doing that to him," Alani's overly dramatic ass shrieked.

"Well, as long as he stays a good boy and not a fuck nigga, we good. I even got Diamond to

EllaSoul Productions

reattach his dreads, so he'll be alright," I shrugged, unbothered.

"Girl, you're crazy as hell! And to think I had the nerve to think that I be tripping on Adonis but he got it made compared to what you be putting Rock through," Envy added and we all laughed.

"Man, I love Rock, but I'm not dumb. As soon as I let up on him, I know that he'll think shit sweet and that's not the case at all. I cook, clean, fuck 'em good, I'm his biggest supporter, and I'm the realest nigga on his team. I'll go to war for my nigga – he mine for life and I'm not letting his ass go, believe that."

For the rest of the time we were there, we just sat and talked about life, love, and business. I tried to control the urges I had to spaz out on Rock, but sometimes they get the best of me cause when they do, nothing good comes from the situation.

Something in my head was always telling me to do something and when it did, I couldn't control it. I had to act out on the scenes that popped into my head. I had to and would protect myself at all costs. Not even just physically, but mentally as well.

EllaSoul Productions

Chapter 18

Rock

♫ On Remy straight tonight dog no chaser ♫

"This your last night as a single man – how you feeling my nigga?" I asked Khan.

I'd rented out Envy's club to throw my boy a bachelor party. I had three stripper poles installed sporadically throughout the club, I'd recruited some of the baddest bitches, and paid for an open bar. I knew that if Envy could see how I had turned her spot out she'd kill me.

One of the women walking around for bottle service stopped by to drop off another bottle of Hennessey for me and my boys. Me, Khan, and Adonis had our own section while some of our corner boys along with a few of the niggas on Adonis' label floated around, tossing money at the strippers.

There was pussy popping everywhere. If my girl wasn't half past crazy, I would definitely have one, if not two of these hoes spread eagle in my hotel room, popping that pussy for a real nigga.

"Man, I feel good, yo. She's my everything. I've done a lot of grimy shit in my life, especially to her and she done stuck it out with a nigga through it all. I honestly couldn't ask for more. She done been down with a nigga from the shine through the struggle. But fuck all that, you knew that shit already, and you got me sounding like some punk bitch," he laughed. "But for real my nigga, when you gone make an honest woman out of Bam loony ass?" He asked me.

I ran my hand over my face and sipped my drink before answering him.

"Man, that's my lil' baby don't get me wrong, but Bam is a fucking maniac."

Khan and Adonis laughed like I was joking or some shit.

"Nigga I know lil' sis a firecracker, but she can't be that bad," Khan replied laughing so hard he spilled his drink.

"Can't be that bad? She's so fucking unhinged and it's only gotten worse since she's been pregnant. Y'all think this shit is funny. Yo, check this. So one night I got held up at the trap, but I called her to let her know what was up; it ain't like she isn't aware of the type of business I conduct out in these streets. Shit, she be out there with me so of course she knows what time it is. Anyway, so I get home once I'm done and she's up reading on her kindle and shit. So I take a shower, eat, get some pussy and go to sleep. You would think everything

95

is good considering the fact she let a nigga hit, right? WRONG!

"Man, I wake up the next morning to something moving up my leg. I'm just thinking that Bam's extra horny ass want some dick. I feel something by my dick and something just told me to flip back the comforter and open my eyes. It's a fucking big ass Albino Python with its head right by my dick flicking its tongue out and shit.

I'm not even going to front, I started screaming like a lil' bitty bitch, yelling her name and shit. Man, this bitch come up in the room butt naked, smiling with a whole tray of food. I'm like 'bitch get this fucking snake' then she gone have the fucking nerve to say, 'I bet you come home at a reasonable time next time,' then walked out. I was so fucking pissed, but I knew that I had to calm down to get that fucking snake off me"

Khan and Adonis were cracking the fuck up – they were laughing so hard they had doubled over.

"So bruh... you trying to tell me that you were about to get some head from a damn snake?" Khan asked me.

"Shut the fuck up nigga! Fuck you."

"Alright nigga get your panties out a bunch. What happened next?" Adonis asked.

"After I got that bitch off me I put it back in the cage and went downstairs. Then, I grabbed her by her fucking hair, bent her over the sink while she was washing dishes, and fucked the dog shit outta her lil' sexy, feisty ass."

"Bruh, y'all wild as shit."

"Yeah but she keep a nigga grounded and on his toes at the same time."

EllaSoul Productions

Chapter 19

Brooke

Can you tell me how can one miss what she's never had?

How can I reminisce when there is no past?

How could I have memories of being happy with you boy?

Can someone tell me how could this be?

I was sitting in the dark nursing some cranberry juice vibing to Tamia's song, *Almost.* It was as if she was singing about my life. I was scrolling down Facebook, looking at a crap-ton of posts about Alani and Khan getting married. I didn't even realize that I was crying until my tears started blurring my vision and finding their resting place on the screen of my phone.

I'd successfully distanced myself away from everybody and started focusing on myself. I knew that I needed to get my shit together. I was losing myself in a man that didn't even want my ass. I knew I needed to tighten up, so I took a step back and started working on Brooke. So, I found me a little job at Wal-Mart, and moved out of my old place. I'd found a nice, small, and modest two-bedroom rancher; it was in foreclosure, so I got it at a decent price. Instead of blowing all the money that

Khan had been giving me over the years, I'd been saving it for a rainy day.

I knew the day would come sooner or later, but I was grateful that I'd prepared for it. I didn't want anyone to know where I was so that I could grieve my lost love on my own terms. I'd been doing great until I caught wind of their wedding invitations where he's holding her very pregnant belly and looking at her with so much love in his eyes. They looked so happy and that's the happiness I wanted for myself. Once I saw that, all of my emotions came rushing back.

Fuck this juice. I ran to the kitchen and grabbed a bottle of wine. I poured me a glass but left it on the counter and drank straight from the bottle. I was going to this wedding if it was the last damn thing I did. They were about to feel my wrath and regret fucking me over.

Chapter 20

Alani

♫ Beneath the sight of God, I will make this vow to you ♫

"Sit your ass still before your shit be all fucked up," Diamond scolded me.

I'd paid her a pretty penny to come out to slay my wedding party's hair and beat all our faces.

"I'm trying to," I responded, when in reality, however, my nerves were through the roof. The day had finally come for me to jump the broom with the only man I'd ever loved.

Khan getting his act together showed me that he was serious about our relationship. I hadn't been trapping at all since I got pregnant; I only snuck and did drops, counts, or checked out books from time to time. Khan has been doing what I hadn't been able to do, and he still made it home at a reasonable hour each night. But now was the time that we took our relationship to the next level and it'd been a long time coming.

It felt as if my baby was doing somersaults in my stomach, which only added to my anxiety.

"I'm about to go smoke me a blunt. Somebody talk to her ass," Diamond said walking out of the dressing room. Envy came and rubbed my back, sitting down next to me.

"It's going to be okay, baby. I was the same way when me and Adonis tied the knot. You spend all this money and time planning and it's over in a maximum of twenty minutes," Envy said laughing and I joined in.

"Thank you, boo. I really needed to hear that," I thanked her.

"No problem, that's what I'm here for."

Envy's words were reassuring but did little to ease my mind or racing heart. I couldn't help but to feel as if this was only the calm before the storm and something was going to ruin my big day. Diamond came back into the room a little mellower.

"Are you ready now, bitch?" She asked me with her hand resting upon her tiny hip. Diamond was like five-feet tall at max and she had a baby face. Most people thought she was a little girl even though she's a grown ass woman. Some men have even asked her for her ID before attempting to get her number while we were out partying.

"Yes, let's get this shit over and done with," I replied matching her attitude, even though it was all love between us. Once Diamond finished my hair and did our faces, she left to go get dressed for my wedding.

"Alright now, we got thirty minutes until show time, so you bitches need to be ready," my self-proclaimed wedding planner Mama Megan came in and told everyone, holding her clipboard.

"We ready, Ma! You ain't got to yell" Bam said, getting up.

"Girl don't make me fuck yo' little ass up, pregnant or not," Megan yelled.

"Alright, Ma, chill out. Go make sure everything else is in place, we'll be ready," I stated, attempting to intervene.

"Whatever," was her reply while leaving out of the dressing room.

"Her ass goes from zero to one hundred real quick," Bam said laughing.

I couldn't understand for the life of me why she gets a kick out of fucking with Megan's ass. If you ask me it's because they are one and the same – both of them have a couple screws loose.

If I hadn't stopped them, they probably would still be going at it. They fuss like it's nobody's business.

"Come on y'all, let's get this shit over with. I feel like I could go into labor at any moment the way this little mutha' fucka jumping around," I told everybody.

We all made sure there was nothing out of place and then got in place. I was having my wedding at the Botanical Gardens and everything was gorgeous. All my anxiety was replaced with a feeling of euphoria. I didn't think there was anything that could bring me down from the high that I was feeling. The music started to play and I walked down the aisle to Avant and KeKe Wyatt's, *You & I.*

I watched as Bam, Rock, Envy, and Adonis all walked down and took their places alongside Khan and where I would soon be. When it was time for me to walk down the aisle, I couldn't contain it anymore and started crying. I think it took me to getting knocked up for Khan to take our relationship completely seriously... and I couldn't be happier.

It's official, I'm Mrs. Khan Thomas. Walking back down the aisle hand in hand with my love was the greatest feeling. Our nuptials went off without a hitch... Or so I thought.

"Well congratulations, Mr. and Mrs. Thomas," Brooke stated vindictively.

The only thing running through my mind was how the fuck she got in here without anyone noticing. Oh, and the fact the she was sporting a pregnant belly that looked as if she was due any day now.

"Bitch, just because it's my day, I'm going to give you a pass and let you walk out here without

103

having to pick your fucking face up off the damn floor," I sneered in her direction as Khan held me back.

"Oh, is that anyway to talk to your sister wife?" she laughed.

"Sister wife?" I asked incredulously.

"Yes, this little boy here," she said, rubbing her belly, "means that we'll be bonded for life. And this guy here," she said, pointing to Khan, "is the common denominator."

"Brooke carry yo' ass with that bullshit," Khan finally spoke up since the beginning of this whole ordeal.

"Well, I figured now was as good of time as any to share the good news. Now that you guys are married, we can all be one big happy family," she replied.

"Oh hell naw, bitch I know that you better pick your big nasty ass up and get the fuck out of here. I'm telling you now this here ain't what you want," Mama Megan said getting up and coming over to where we were with a pissed off Bam in tow.

It didn't even occur to me that all eyes were on us.

EllaSoul Productions

"Nasty? Who you calling nasty?" Brooke asked like Megan could have been possibly talking to anybody else.

"You, bitch. You look nasty with that little ass dress on making you look like a pig in a fucking blanket. You look like twelve pounds of potato salad stuffed into a six-pound bag coming in here showing out. You're just trashy and distasteful. Get yo' life," Megan read her ass and I couldn't help but to laugh.

"What you laughing at, bitch?" She snapped in my direction.

Before I could even respond Bam hopped on her ass, then Megan jumped in on that ass, then Envy, and the last person I expected, Khanna. Khan ran over to try and break it up, along with Adonis and Rock. I took that as my moment to get a few licks in. I wanted to get that bitch for the good, the bad, and the ugly. Once they had successfully got everybody else off her, they tried to get me off, but I was still tagging that ass.

I delivered blow after blow to her face for every time she played on my phone, every time she deliberately fucked my man, and every time she had any hand in causing me pain. When they finally got me off that hoe, my entire white gown was drenched in her blood. We all got up and left, leaving her stretched out on the floor. Besides, I did have a reception to get to after all.

Her being pregnant didn't matter to me one iota. She ought to have known that coming to my wedding on some humbug shit wasn't going to end pretty. If you ask me, she put herself at risk by being the messy bitch that she is.

EllaSoul Productions

Chapter 21

Brooke

♫ I heard church bells ringing ♫

Okay, I know that I said that I wasn't going to do anything else to deliberately try and hurt their relationship, but why should they be happy and get to be one big happy family while me and my son were left to fend for ourselves? My intentions were to just make my presence known and to let them know that I was with child since I had been ducked off my entire pregnancy.

But seeing her elated and smiling with a life that I believe should be mine pissed me off. They had a bitch sitting there feeling like Etta James. Now the last thing I expected was for them to all beat my ass like that, especially when Khanna jumped in because we were once thick as thieves. Maybe she found out I fucked her man back before I found out I was pregnant, but that's neither here nor there.

While they were fucking me up, I just laid in the fetal position trying to protect my stomach. I wish I would've just shut my ass up cause now I'd put my son's life in jeopardy. Again, I was in a fucked-up situation behind Khan's dumb ass. I don't know how long they beat me up, but I woke up in the hospital. I felt my stomach and it wasn't completely flat, but it was smaller than it should have been.

EllaSoul Productions

I started going crazy trying to rip the IV's out of my arm. The monitors started going off and two nurses and a doctor came rushing in.

"Ms. Walker calm down."

"Fuck calming down, where the fuck is my damn son?" I screamed on the verge of having a fucking conniption.

"He's fine. He's fine, we just need you to calm down."

That eased my mind a little bit, so I sat back while the nurses reattached my IV and the monitors.

The uneasy look on the doctor's face raised my suspicion

"Can I see my baby?" I asked him with a raised eyebrow.

"Ms. Walker, my name is Dr. Calhoun. You came in here pretty banged up. If it was a minute later, your son could have died. We gave you an emergency C-Section, but your son was hemorrhaged and lost a lot of blood. We've already checked, and you are not a match. Is there any way that you could contact his father and get him to donate some blood? He's stable for now, but we are going to need some blood for a transfusion for him as soon as possible."

EllaSoul Productions

The wheels in my head immediately started turning. I was going to make it my business to make them motherfuckers hurt for causing harm to my seed. I just needed Khan to donate some blood for my baby boy first. Once I knew for sure that he was straight, I could put my plan in motion.

"Ms. Walker did you hear me?" Dr. Calhoun asked me.

"Um yes, I can call his father to donate blood. He should be a match indefinitely since I'm not, but can I go see him and name him?" I asked him.

"Yes, we'll wheel you right down there," he replied going to get me a wheelchair.

I was going to make them wish they had never fucked with a bitch like me.

Chapter 22

Khanna

You ain't no friend of mine

Fuck Brooke's hoe ass. That bitch must've thought I wasn't going to find out about her fucking my nigga Dae-Dae. I'd been fucking with Dae'Sean Britt for years now. That nigga was my first everything, but we had an on again-off again relationship. I was doing me, and he was doing him, so there were really no hard feelings. So, one day we were sitting around talking and decided to put all our shit out there since we were on again.

It was then that he confessed to fucking Brooke when she all but made him fall in the pussy. Not saying that he was right or wrong, but with her being my best friend, she knew that nigga was off limits. It's just an unspoken code that you don't fuck with your best friend's man. He wasn't just some nigga who had been tricking off on me, he was bae. I forgave him, and hopefully it isn't a mistake. But as for me and her being cool ever again, it was a done deal, over, finito.

Since she basically all but dropped off the face of the earth, I'd been getting closer to Alani and Bam. With them expecting children with my brother and cousin, they were practically family. To my surprise, they were cool as shit, and Bam was hilarious. It actually made me feel some type of way

110

that I spent all this time hating them for no particular reason at all.

We had been bonding and, even though I knew we weren't gonna be besties overnight, it felt good to at least be on speaking terms with them.

Brooke's ass only got what she deserved. You can't keep doing people dirty and expect for Karma to not come back and bite you in the ass. As far as I was concerned, revenge is a dish best served cold.

"Bae, you home?" I heard Dae yell out.

"Yeah, I'm upstairs," I responded.

After the fiasco at the wedding, I went home to shower and change since I had Brooke's blood on me.

"Damn, girl! All this ass, you bouta' make me have to slide up in this shit real quick," Dae-Dae said walking up behind me while I put lotion on my legs. He gripped my ass and started rubbing my slippery mound.

"Move, boy, I gotta get dressed so I can get to Alani's reception," I said although I didn't bother to put up any resistance.

Dae'Sean knew that shit too because he stuck his finger in my pussy and I started grinding on it. A moan slipped out of my mouth and he took that as his cue. I didn't realize he had already stepped out of his pants until he slid into me.

Dae-Dae started stroking me, slow at first, but I was in need of some long and strong dick. I started throwing my ass into him and he just held onto my hips. I pushed him back on the bed and straddled him, then I guided his eight inches into me and rode him for dear life. I grabbed his hands and placed one on my hip while I placed the other on my breast.

Dae'Sean was a lil' nigga, and by that, I mean he only weighs like 135, at the max. He's skinny and I'm more dominant than him. In our sex sessions, I'm usually leading and taking control, which was fine with me; I know what I like and all that I had to do is tell him to do it and direct him.

I turned around so that I could ride him reverse cowgirl. He slapped my ass and that did nothing but make me go even harder. I jumped up and planted my feet into the mattress. I bucked my hips at him and took one hand to rub and massage my clit, and the other to rub his balls.

That shit drove him crazy. Dae'Sean grabbed my hips and started fucking the shit out of me.

"I'm bouta bust bae," he moaned.

"I'm right behind you!" I screamed as I came all over him.

112

I grabbed a rag to wash him off, then I headed back to the shower.

"Baby I'm out, I got some shit to take care of," Dae came into the bathroom and kissed me.

"Alright boo, I'm bouta head to the reception," I replied kissing him back.

I didn't bother to ask him where he was going because didn't nobody want Dae-Dae except my ass.

EllaSoul Productions

Chapter 23

Khan

♫ I don't know why I be making her feel this way, I ain't even smooth with my bull shit I do it right in her face ♫

Besides the little set-back at our wedding, the reception was going great. We had all gone home to shower and change and met back up at Chic Lounge, where our reception was being held. Despite Brooke showing her ass, Alani was acting as if nothing had happened.

We had our first dance as husband and wife, and now we were just chilling with our closest friends and family. I couldn't help but let my mind wander to Brooke. I wondered if her baby was mine and if so, if she and the baby were okay. But for the time being, I would just enjoy being in the company of my love. This time tomorrow, we would be on the white sands of Turks and Cacaos.

"Well, congrats you two."

I turned around to see Shaunda standing there with a smug look on her face and just knew that this wasn't going to be good. I didn't even know how the hell she got in here. Our reception consisted of a more intimate setting compared to our wedding.

114

"If you had at least tried to sound sincere, I would say thank you," Alani clapped back.

"Well, I actually can't really say that I am," Shaunda replied.

"Then why the fuck are you even here?" Alani asked with her temperature rising every second.

"Well, I just thought that you should see what kind of man you have on your hands," Shaunda laughed like she was getting a kick out of this whole ordeal.

I knew that it was time for me to try and diffuse the situation before this shit ended up a bloody massacre like earlier.

"Shaunda, get the fuck out," I growled, yoking her up.

"Oh I'll get out... but not until I show my good friend Alani something," Shaunda said snatching away from me and pulling out her phone.

If La'La didn't leave me earlier, I knew for sure that she was going to leave my dumb ass now. I snatched Shaunda's phone and looked at the screen and there was a video of me fucking the shit out of her. Someone had zoomed in on my dick giving a full view of the fact like I was raw dogging her.

I looked at Alani's face and it held no emotion. I didn't know what to do or say because I didn't know how she was feeling. Before I could react, Bam flew across the room knocking Shaunda over the head with a fucking bottle. As if my day couldn't get any worse.

"What the fuck, Sophie? You pregnant as hell and this yo' second time fighting in the same fucking day," Rock said snatching Bam up.

"Ayo Don, help me get this bitch the fuck out of here," I called out to Adonis while pointing to Shaunda.

Once we were done, I came back inside and my mama pulled me to the side.

"Fix this shit, now! I taught yo' dumb ass way better than this," she said mushing me in my head.

"I know, Ma! That's what I'm about to go do now," I replied and left to go search for Alani.

When I spotted her, she was laughing and joking around with Bam, Envy, and Khanna.

"Bae, can I holla at you for a minute?" I said grabbing her arm, but the cold look in Bam's eyes caused me to let go.

"No need to explain; let's just have fun and enjoy our big day. After all, we did just get

116

married," she said standing to kiss my lips as she pulled the bottom one in between her teeth.

I looked in her eyes to try and read her but saw nothing. I was going to let it go for now, but we would talk about this later when we got home. I don't know how I fucked up and gave Shaunda some dick. The fucked-up part about it was that it was the night of the baby shower. I'd always knew that she wanted me, even back in the day when we were youngins.

I used to let her suck my dick from time to time, but then I wanted to try and do right by La'La so I put an end to it. One day, we had a selling party 'round the way and she was there. One thing led to another and I was balls deep in that shit. Ever since then, she'd been addicted to the D. I tried cutting the bitch off a billion times, but she always came running back.

That's why I told La'La to stop hanging with her trick ass. I had been doing well by Alani until she brought her hot twat around. At the end of the day, I'm still a man and you can only turn down a ready and willing pussy for so long. I took that bitch home after that shit between her Alani and Bam, and it was all she wrote after that.

If only I could turn back the hands of time and right all my wrongs against Alani, I would, but something was telling me that it was too late. She

117

wouldn't get away from me easily this time, though because I put a ring on that pretty little finger of hers and popped a baby off in her ass.

I woke up the next morning with a hangover out of this world, I was drinking like a fish last night and now I was paying the ultimate price. I reached over to pull La'La close to me only to find her side of the bed empty. I figured that she had went out to buy some last-minute things for our honey moon. I went down stairs, opened the microwave and found a plate of food with a note attached to it.

Dear Khan,

It's weird to be writing you a letter, but I know that had I tried to tell you face to face, you would have never let me leave. Yesterday should have been one of the happiest days of my life, but with your selfish actions, you've once again caused me a great deal of pain. I've stuck beside you through it all, the bitches and the secret abortions that you think I know nothing about, but the straw that breaks the camel's back is you having outside children on me.

You've let someone give you something that only I was supposed to. She could be possibly birthing not only your first child, but your first son, and that is something that I just cannot stomach. I'm far from stupid, but I can shamefully admit that I have been a complete fool for you. I've turned a blind eye to all of the fucked up shit that you have done to me. I thought that if I stuck around, showed you how down I was for you, how deep my loyalty ran, how much I loved you, and how I am the one for you, you would one day make all the suffering I went through because of you worthwhile. But each time I forgave you, you lost a little more respect for me. No one can love someone who allows themselves to be disrespected. By allowing you to walk all over me, I actually stunted your growth by not forcing you to change.

Men can only love strong women who know their worth and don't settle for less because those are the women who make them better men. The person you are weak for will never love you... that is until you become strong for somebody else. But how can you love me when you haven't really learned to love yourself? What I thought was my knight in shining armor turned out to be a mirage. You've hurt me time and time again, now enough is enough.

Even now with me leaving you, I still put you first by pausing to make your breakfast. The truth is you just aren't man enough for me. I could have gotten over you fucking Shaunda because I know she is a whole THOTianna and probably threw the shit at you, but what I can't excuse is you fucking her the day of my baby shower. Honestly, how disrespectful can you be? I don't even think I want to know the answer to that. Don't come looking for me, I'll be in contact with you.

119

Sincerely,

Your biggest regret!

I threw the plate of food against the wall and watched it shatter, I'd completely lost my appetite. They say a man ain't supposed to cry and I was feeling like a certified bitch the way the tears just cascaded down my face. I'd finally lost her and there was absolutely nothing I could do about it.

EllaSoul Productions

Chapter 24

Khan

♫ I really messed up, can you call me back ♫

I had just gotten back to the states, but I wasn't feeling refreshed at all. There was a piece of me missing and I probably wouldn't feel better until I got my girl back.

"Baby you okay? You look like you're stressed about something," Shaunda asked rubbing my clenching jaw.

Yeah, I know I shouldn't have taken her on a trip that was reserved for me and Alani, but I needed to get away and I didn't want to be left alone. So, I hit Shaunda up and told her to meet me at the airport. She didn't have a passport but the nigga I knew that worked in customs let us slide. Everything in the house we once shared reminded me of Alani and I couldn't face it. She had left all of her belongings behind and the entire house still smelled like her favorite Daisy perfume.

I'd been staying at Shaunda's house since we touched down, and now I was taking her to a doctor's appointment. Yeah you guessed it, this bitch is pregnant. I could possibly have three kids on the way, by three different women, might I add. I knocked Shaunda's hand away.

121

"Bitch, I told you about that baby shit and don't fucking touch me," I spazed out on her.

Sensing I wasn't in the mood, she left me alone. There was only one bitch that walked the face of this earth that could call me baby, and that was the same bitch that left me the day after our wedding. When we pulled up to the doctor's office, I cut the car off and hopped out walking towards the building.

"Damn, hold the fuck up," Shaunda called herself snapping, jumping out of the car trying to keep up with my quick strides. Instead of responding, I retrieved my ringing phone from my pocket.

"Talk to me," I answered the phone for Rock.

"Yo I know you and La'La ain't on good terms or whatever, but I just thought that you should know that she's in labor with your Shorty," he told me all in one breath.

"Good looks bruh," I said hanging up and hitting an about face.

"What the fuck, Khan?! Did you forget that I have a fucking appointment?" Shaunda stressed, trying to catch up to me.

"Shut the fuck up and either ride or get the fuck out," I stated matter-of-factly.

EllaSoul Productions

To my surprise, she hopped right in the passenger seat. I drove 80MPH all the way to Norfolk's Main Hospital. I didn't need to ask what hospital she was in because I already knew where her doctor was.

When pulled up, I didn't even bother to park, I just tossed the keys to the valet. I ran to the elevator as soon as I found out where the labor and delivery room was located. I checked my phone to see that Rock had texted me her room number. I ran in and there was Dr. Calhoun, a nurse, my mother, Alani, Bam, Khanna, and Envy.

All eyes were on me.

"See now Khan, you trying my fucking patience. Get the fuck out before I make you regret your very existence," Bam said through clenched teeth, looking like she wanted to take my head off. I looked behind me – just that quick I had forgotten that I even had Shaunda with me. I could kick my own ass for that shit.

I made eye contact with Alani and her eyes held no emotion. I'd lost my baby for real y'all.

"Go sit in the car or the waiting room," I told Shaun 'cause there was no way in hell that I was missing the birth of my shorty. She looked like she wanted to say something but decided against it when Alani's goon squad gave her the death stare.

123

"Alright Ms. Clarke, get ready to push," Dr. Calhoun told Alani.

I wanted to correct that nigga and tell him her last name was Thomas but decided not to. I walked over to the right side of her bed, I rubbed her face and was pleasantly surprised when she didn't slap my hand away.

"We're crowning now. On your next contraction, I want you to give me one big push," he coached her.

"You got this baby," I told her reassuringly and kissed her forehead that was damp with perspiration.

"Alright, one big push."

I watched as my baby girl pushed with all her might. After five minutes of pushing, the baby was out.

"And here you have a beautiful baby girl. Do you want to cut the cord, dad?" Dr. Calhoun asked me.

I just nodded my head "yeah" and walked forward. I cut the cord and they shuffled the baby away to clean and weigh her while they sewed up her mother.

"So, what are you gonna name her?" I asked Alani while she looked in my daughter's eyes. But

124

before she could respond, someone busted through the door.

"Bae, I got here as fast as I could. Did you have my baby yet?" Some random ass nigga said running into the room. We made eye contact and that's all I remember before I went berserk and everything went black.

EllaSoul Productions

Chapter 25

Alani

♫ Tell me are you that somebody ♫

I know what y'all thinking that only some slut would be throwing that ass at some nigga while she's pregnant with another nigga baby and technically a newlywed. But Rich was just a friend… for now. I met him one day while I was going to Starbucks before I started shopping for my new condo. Leaving Khan was the hardest thing that I've ever had to do.

When I left Khan, I left everything except the clothes on my back and my purse. I knew I probably shouldn't have caffeine, but I knew I had a long day ahead of me. Rich walked up on me while I was ordering my venti iced white chocolate mocha with an extra shot of espresso, extra whipped cream and caramel.

"Umm, that will be decaf," he said to the cashier just as I was about to pay.

"Excuse the fuck out of you," I snapped in his direction.

"Baby girl, you don't need to be drinking all that caffeine while you pregnant with my baby."

Before I could even respond, he paid, they called my order, and he snatched it (and me) up.

126

I snatched my drink from him, went to sit at a table all by my lonesome, and left him standing there. Being pregnant had me so emotional to the point I just started crying as soon as my ass hit the seat. He came over to me.

"You should never have to cry over a nigga. I got you baby, and you'll never have to cry again."

After that, it was all she wrote. He'd helped me with the furnishing of my condo and a new wardrobe. I had plenty of money saved up and even if I never worked or hustled another day in my life, me and my baby would be straight. But shit, he was offering so I was accepting. He had always been the perfect gentleman and had never pressured me to do anything. I'd always tried to correct him when he calls my baby his, but he insisted so eventually, I just stopped and let it go. Rich knew just like I knew that he was not my child's real father.

Snapping back to the matter at hand.

"I know good and got damn well y'all dumb asses ain't in here humbugging and I got my fucking daughter right here. Y'all niggas tripping."

Here we were, my ass getting patched the fuck up, and they wanna fight. Security bum rushed the room and these niggas were still going at it. Security tried to break them up but were having a hard time. They didn't stop until Bam pulled out a taser and zapped both of their asses.

127

"Get the fuck out!" I screamed.

Khan and Rich just looked at each other waiting for the other to move.

"Both of y'all get the fuck out."

They both just dropped their heads in shame and moved towards the door. Out of nowhere, the hospital room door burst open yet again. You're probably thinking it was the police but guess again.

"I been looking for you for the fucking longest nigga. My fucking son in here fighting for his damn life and you act like you too good to answer the fucking phone," Brooke shouted at Khan as she started crying.

In a brief second, I felt for her, but quickly shook that off thinking of all the shit she'd put me through. That ass whooping was coming to her sooner or later. This shit was too much and I wanted to cry but I had no more tears left, at least not for this dog ass nigga. Something has got to give.

EllaSoul Productions

Chapter 26

Khan

♫ I guess I gotta live with the fact I did you wrong forever ♫

Seeing the lost and far off look in Alani's eyes and the tears streaming down Brooke's face broke me. I felt less of a man. Since the wedding when I found out that Brooke was pregnant, I knew that there was a possibility that her baby was mine, but in some weird way, I felt like if I didn't think about it that it would go away. I looked into La'La's face, then back at Brooke, and walked out... but not before she snuffed my ass.

"You stupid bitch, I hate yo' muthafucking ass!" Brooke yelled, fucking me up.

Lil' Speedy, one of my runners, came from nowhere and scooped her up taking her out the room. She broke away from him and came back to me.

"Go give some blood to your fucking son before you wish you never met me," she said in almost whisper. And with that, she walked out. I couldn't do shit but go to the NICU and check out this kid to see if he was mine.

Chapter 27

Rich

♫ Yeah that's my baby, no Beyoncé or Jay-Z ♫

Damn I'm pissed the fuck off that I missed my shawty giving birth to my seed. I didn't give a fuck what the fuck DNA had to say, I'm a grown ass man and know that if I want a woman with kids, her children are a package deal. So hell yeah I claimed Lil' Mama's seed! I knew she was still in love with her bitch ass husband, but I was willing to be right there when she finally came around.

I'm a different kind of nigga when it comes down to my lil' mama so I know she was a little thrown off seeing me humbugging in her hospital room. Her husband might've left but I damn sure wasn't about to leave. I stepped out of the room to give her some space, but I was definitely going back in.

I didn't even get to see baby girl. The only reason I knew it was a girl is because I heard La'La when she said daughter. I wondered what she was gonna name her, but eventually said "fuck wondering" and turned around to go find out.

When I walked back into the room, everybody was standing around Alani's bed ogling over the baby. She had her biological father's skin

130

complexion, but everything else came from Alani. She was flat-out gorgeous. I walked over and kissed Alani's forehead and did the same with the baby.

"Her name is Karizma," she told me, and it matched her perfectly.

I felt someone staring at me, so I turned around and locked eyes with her best friend, Bam. I knew who she was from me and Alani's many conversations and the numerous pictures around her condo.

"How are you guys doing? I've heard nothing but great things about y'all," I said to everyone in the room. The only person to speak back was her friend Envy.

"Well we can't say the same for you," her "Mother in-law" said exuding too much attitude. "Well, I'm Richard, but everyone calls me Rich for starters," I spoke still trying my hand at being polite.

"I don't give a damn about none of that shit. What the fuck is up with you claiming my grandchild? She already has a father, so you can get the fuck out of here with your bullshit."

I wasn't feeling her tone of voice and figured it'd be best for me to get the fuck on before I said some shit to hurt her feelings.

"I'll be back through later Lil' Mama. Stay up," I said kissing her and walking out. I had some business to take care of anyway. The last thing I was about to do was kiss the ass of woman I gave less than a fuck about. Plus, I wasn't in the business of explaining myself to anybody. I'd just come back to check La'La later.

Walking out to my car, I couldn't help but feel a presence behind me, so I turned around. When I turned around, I was looking down the barrel of gun. I always think on my feet, and in my line of business you have to be ready and prepared for everything.

"I wish that we didn't have to meet like this," I chuckled at Bam.

"This here ain't a social call. What are your intentions with my sister?" She asked with a scowl on her face.

I thought it was the cutest thing: her thugged out exterior and protruding belly. She had a baby face that made her look as if she's twelve and she was so short standing at only four-foot-eleven.

"That's my future," was my simple reply.

I could see her checking my eyes for any kind of deception. I'm guessing she found none because she started to back away but never lowered her strap.

132

"I'm watching you," she said as she disappeared as quickly as she came.

EllaSoul Productions

Chapter 28

Khan

As I look into my son's eyes, I had to admit that I was smitten. Just in case you're wondering, yes, Brooke's son is my son. This lil' nigga looked just like me. He was most definitely my twin, but the blood test that needed to be taken to see if I was a match only confirmed it. Khan Raleigh Thomas, Jr. was definitely my seed.

I planned on being the best father I could be to both of my kids. My father, Kane, walked out on my mother when I was five and Khanna was three. My mother gave us no explanation as to why he left. When I was thirteen, she told us he died. Khanna and my mama went to the funeral, but I had absolutely no reason to go. That nigga didn't mean shit to me then and he still doesn't now. He just gave me the motivation I needed to be a great father to my kids.

Don't get me wrong, I loved my son already, but I just wished that Brooke wasn't his mother. I know that this has destroyed any chances that me and my wife have of getting back together. Shaunda called herself being pissed at a nigga because I told her to take her ass home while I handled all my business. I just wanted to spend time with the both of my children and I couldn't do that with her breathing down my fucking neck.

134

Brooke hadn't put me through any bullshit since the blood test for my Jr. came back, but that didn't mean I'd missed the cold look in her eyes. She looked off, but every time I ask her about it she just says that it's nothing or ignores me completely. I didn't know how I allowed my life to become this convoluted. I went from having it all to having absolutely nothing. I mean, I still had money and the business was running smoothly, but what is success without someone to share it with?

I know that I could have my pick of the litter when it comes to getting women, but none of them bitches would ever have anything on Alani. Now, here I was with two kids and possibly one on the way; no bitch in her right mind would want a nigga after that. Even though I would love to be with La'La, I know that shit will never be the same. She'd never look at me the same, she'd never love me the same, and all of my past indiscretions would continuously be on the forefront of her mind.

I'd ruined her and there was nothing that I could do about it.

EllaSoul Productions

Chapter 29

Alani

♫ You're everything to me, you're the air that I breathe, the song I sing... ♫

Today was the day that baby Karizma and I got to go home and I hadn't seen Khan since the day I had Kay-Kay. So, as always, it was Rich to the rescue taking us home. In only a short period of time, he had shown me how a real man was supposed to treat a lady. I'd never even attempted to put him and Khan into the same category because Rich has always treated me with the utmost respect.

I'd only been with one man in my entire life and that was Khan, so I didn't have much experience when it came down to men. But that Rich, baybee, believe me when I tell you that man makes me feel so alive, and we haven't even been intimate.

Each day, the distance grew between me and Khan while I got closer to Rich. I'm not going to lie and say that I don't still love him because I do, but I refused to continue to be a fool for him. I'd allowed him to make a spectacle of me one too many times. A love child is just something that I cannot accept. I won't be the bird brain ass bitch with a man who has more outside children than he has with his wife.

Fool me once shame on you, fool me twice then shame on me. I had been bamboozled by him too many times to even count. You often hear people say that love hurts but that was the biggest lie I'd ever heard. Love doesn't hurt; the lies, the betrayal, the cheating, the deceit, and a love lost is what hurts. There is no greater feeling than being loved on by someone with a beautiful soul.

As we made it to my condo, Rich carried all of the baby's things into her room while I carried the car seat. When I reached her nursery, I saw that he had painted it, and bought tons of gender specific clothing. He had removed all of the unisex things that were bought and replaced it all with customized things. The entire nursery was purple, black and, white. Her bassinette had Karizma engraved on the side, the wall also had her name on it, and he had a purple K hanging on the outside of her door.

"Aww baby, when did you even have time to do all of this? I wasn't even in the hospital that long," I asked him in complete shock. "Don't worry about all that. Do you like it?" He asked me.

"Do I like it? I love it, boo!" I screamed jumping up to kiss him. Initially I didn't want a relationship with Rich because I'd met him as a single newlywed. Yeah, I know, that shit sounds crazy as fuck… but he has me wrapped in a whirlwind of love that makes it hard not to want to be in his presence.

137

In the short amount of time that Karizma has been in this world, he has done more for me and her than her own father. Khan doesn't even know her name, but I've heard through the grapevine that he is indeed the father of Brooke's child, and that he has been with her and their baby since he walked out of my hospital room days ago.

Even though we aren't together, I always thought that he would do right by our child. I guess it doesn't matter how long you've known somebody because you might not necessarily know them. Hopefully he comes around and soon. I highly doubted that Rich would mind playing a father role to her, but at the end of the day, she needs the guy who helped to create her. I guess only time will tell.

EllaSoul Productions

Chapter 30

Shaunda

♫ Nobody has to know, for you I give it up ♫

As I dry heaved into the toilet for the third time since I woke up this morning, I thought about what I really wanted to do. I hadn't seen Khan since his bitch ass wife had her baby and I'd been sick as a dog since I found out that I was pregnant. I didn't want to share Khan with anybody; I wanted him completely to myself. Why else would I go through so much trouble to break him and Alani up? I could've shown her the footage I'd secretly recorded of us fucking the night of her baby shower long before I did. I thought it would be better if I waited though and showed her on her wedding day.

That way if she ever thought about taking him back and their anniversary came, she would always have to think about his infidelity. Khan had always let pussy cloud his judgment and despite his thuggish exterior, he was really a sweet guy and I preyed on that. When he dropped me off at home that night, I faked like I was feeling worse than I really was so he could see me into the house. He laid me down and asked me if needed anything. I took that as my cue to take what I really needed… him.

I went straight for his belt buckle and before he could protest, his dick was in my mouth. I was

139

sucking like my life depended on it and it did. I needed a new sponsor, and what better guy than someone who I'd been crushing on for years. He grabbed onto the back of my head for leverage.

"Aww fuck Shaun," he groaned and started fucking my face. His balls were slapping my chin while his dick massaged my tonsils, but I was determined not to gag.

One thing I knew for sure was that my head game was official. I started rubbing his balls in a circular motion with one hand and jacking him with the other.

"Damn bitch, just like that," he moaned, tightening the grip that he had on my hair.

I didn't care about him calling me "bitch" because I had him right where I wanted him, and when he busted his nut, I swallowed it all.

I knew that the first thing he would do was go to the bathroom and freshen up so I used that as my time to strike. I used a Sina from Love and Hip-Hop Atlanta move and set the camera and shit up. But instead of chocolate, I had I whole sex swing set in my living room. When he walked out of the bathroom and headed towards the front door, he spotted me.

"Yo, we can't do this shit, Shaun. What just happened is already bad enough," he said still

140

walking toward the door. He threw a stack on money on the coffee table but never stopped his stride.

"Please baby, just let me get a sample and I promise I'll leave you alone for good. It's been years since I last had some and I'm having withdrawals," I said poking out my pouty lips.

I could see him contemplating his decision, so I thought that I would help him out a little bit by massaging him through his pants. Before I knew it, he had me in that swing fucking the dear life up out my little ass.

I was barley in the swing, but I was holding on to the straps while he held my bottom half up with my legs in the crook of his arms.

"Damn baby, just like that," I moaned out in pained pleasure. He had that dope dick which is why I was craving it so bad. He was the only nigga that could make me cum off the dick alone.

Most niggas had to give me some head just so that I could climax, while after others I had to mount a dildo. I loved dick and Khan's was, by far, the best I'd ever had. Hands down, he won the title.

We fucked for the rest of the night to the point where the memory on the camera was full. But I didn't care. I had that nigga right where I wanted him.

141

Chapter 31

Bam

♫ Why you wanna fly black bird you ain't ever gonna fly ♫

Here I was in labor and the stupid ass father of my child was nowhere to be found. My contractions were two minutes apart and I knew that my son was coming soon. I'd tried calling Rock's dumb ass, but he didn't answer the fucking phone. I called La'La, but she didn't answer either, so I left a voice mail.

I was tempted to drive myself until a contraction hit me so hard that I lost my train of thought. I didn't have shit else to do but get myself together and try to deliver my little nigga on my own. I knew I should have gotten a Midwife. I hated hospitals and didn't want to be in there alone.

I filled my Jacuzzi with lukewarm water and grabbed a whole bunch of towels. I got the sharpest pair of scissors I could find and some rubbing alcohol. I stripped from the waist down and tried stepping in but was crippled from the pain. I could feel my baby crowning and knew that I had to try and get him out, and soon.

I finally made it in the tub and sat down. I'd always known, since I became pregnant that I wanted to have a natural water birth. I just wish I

EllaSoul Productions

had someone here to help me, but fuck it, it is what it is.

I paid close attention when Alani had Karizma, so I knew that on my next contraction that I had to push. When I felt it, I pushed with all my might and tried to level my breathing. When I finally delivered my baby, I realized that something was terribly wrong.

EllaSoul Productions

Chapter 32

Alani

I'd just put a colicky and fussy Karizma down for a nap after feeding and changing her. I was so exhausted I figured I would take a nap while she was napping. I checked the time on my phone and saw that I had several missed calls from Bam. I saw that I also had a voicemail from her, so I decided to check that first to see what she wanted. I hadn't seen her much since I had Kay-Kay because I've been busy adjusting to being a new mommy.

When I listened to the voicemail, I screamed for Rich.

"Baby, what's wrong? Why you yelling like that?" he asked with concern etched all over his face. I was throwing on my sneakers while trying to answer him.

"Something is up with Bam. I need to go see about her," I said as I grabbed my purple and black 9mm baby Ruger and checked to make sure it was loaded. "Can you keep an eye on Kay for me 'til I get back?"

"Yeah baby, hand me the baby monitor and call me to let me know what's up," he said kissing my forehead. "Be safe."

"No doubt," I replied walking out the door.

EllaSoul Productions

One thing I loved about Rich is he didn't get in the way of my business. He let me handle shit how I deemed fit and backed me on everything. But right now, Bam was my main concern.

I did 90MPH all the way to her crib, turning a thirty-minute drive into ten. When I got to the house, an eerie felling came over me. I pulled my strap out and call her name.

"Sophie I'm here. Where you at?"

I could hear mumbling coming from the master bathroom so that's where I made my way to. When I got in there, I broke down at the sight before me.

Chapter 33

Rock

When you hurt I hurt too, because even though I fuck up I can't live without you

I woke up and looked at the time on the clock and knew that I had overstayed my welcome. I peeled Margo's naked body off of me and reached for my clothes. Once I was completely dressed, I grabbed my phone and headed for the door. I knew I'd fucked up being over here for so long, but Margo's pussy was addictive. I couldn't sleep without having to keep one eye open, worried about if my baby mama was going to poison me with scorpions and spiders or some shit.

I checked my phone when I got in the car to see that Bam had called me 'bout twenty times.

Not ready to deal with her bullshit, I went to the ABC store to get me a bottle of Henny and rolled me up a few blunts. I took the scenic route home, facing blunt after blunt of Kush the entire way. I knew I was gon' need to be lifted to put up with her line of questioning.

When I pulled up to my block, I could see police, an ambulance, and firetrucks right in front of my crib. I immediately started to think the worst. I hopped out without even properly parking my car.

146

"Hold up son, where do you think you're going?" This Uncle Tom ass cop had the nerve to ask me.

"Fuck off nigga, this my damn crib. My pregnant wife was home when I left," I said with my temperature rising with each passing moment.

The look on his face softened up and before he could say anything else, I saw Bam on the stretcher with a crazed look in her eyes, clutching something to her chest. We locked eyes and I saw nothing, her face was stone and it looked as if she had no soul. I saw a frantic Alani run out of the house covered in blood. Fearing the absolute worst, I ran to her.

"What happened La'La? Please don't tell me something happened to my baby?" I screeched, full of concern. She was too distraught to even answer my question. I ran to the EMT that had put my wifey in the back of the ambulance.

"Yo what happened? That's my wife in there!" I yelled at the EMT.

"Hop in, I'll fill you in on the way."

I got in and shortly after my world came crashing down.

Chapter 34

Khan

"When it's going good it's going great, but when it's bad, it's the worst"

I was checking on the traps, doing count, and making sure everybody had enough work to meet supply and demand when Alani called me. I didn't think I would be hearing from her, but what could I expect when I hadn't even reached out to see my own daughter?

The only reason I knew her name was from when I went back to sign her birth certificate. La'La didn't even know that I went and did it. The last thing I wanted was for her new nigga to think that he was about to sign my seed's shit. I went to see her in the nursery every day before they were released.

"Talk to me," I answered.

"Rock needs you. We're at Sentara," she said into the phone before hanging up.

That was all I needed to hear. I got my lil' nigga Speedy, one of my most trusted workers, to wrap all this shit up, hopped in my Benz, and rushed to see what the fuck was up.

When I walked into the waiting room, I saw my mama, Envy, Adonis, Khanna, Rock, and Alani covered in blood with a faraway look in her eyes. I

148

rushed over to her just to make sure it wasn't coming from her.

"It's not from me," she said as I checked her out, as if she was reading my mind.

Now I was lost. Rock is in the corner, so I knew it wasn't him, my mama and them were good, so who could it be. Right when I was about to go over to Rock, Alani broke down and I grabbed her in my arms to console her and keep her from falling. I was still clueless as to what the fuck was going on, and then it hit me.

"Where's Bam?" I asked her and that only made her cry even harder.

Before I could ask anything else, I heard over my shoulder, "I got it from here, playboy." I turned around and came face to face with the last nigga I wanted to see.

"Nigga, whatever my wife and I got going on ain't got shit to do with you," I growled feeling my temperature rise.

"Nigga, you must mean your soon to be EX-WIFE. Like I said before, I got this, and I hate to repeat myself," he responded with his lil' chest poked out.

I laughed in his face and as if it was on cue the Doctor walked out.

149

"The family of Sophie Young," he said and we all jumped up and walked over.

"We're her family," Alani spoke.

"Well I'm Dr. Chase and I'm sorry to tell you that the baby died during birth. His umbilical cord was wrapped around his neck. I'm still baffled as to how Sophie was able to deliver the baby on her own. She did everything right, but it was already too late. If she would have made it to the hospital in time to deliver, we could have possibly saved him. I'm sorry there was nothing we could do. We were lucky to be able to save Ms. Young, considering the amount of blood she lost. She's going to need a lot of rest. Who will she be going home with?" he asked looking at all of us.

I could see the tears rolling down Rock's face, so Alani spoke up, "With me."

"Well, Ms. Young will be good as new physically, but mentally is a totally different story. I would advise you all to keep a very close eye on her, as this is a very devastating time in her life. She's in room 2103 if you wish to see her. She won't be released until tomorrow. We'd like to keep her overnight for observation."

And with that, he left as quickly as he came.

I went to go grab Rock, but he snatched away from me and punched a hole in the wall and started fucking shit up on his way out of the hospital. I would give him some time to get it all out. I couldn't even attempt to say that I felt where he was coming from because I didn't. All I could do was be there for my nigga in his time of need.

I'd never lost a child a before, and I don't ever want to know the feeling. Karizma and KJ were my life and I honestly couldn't picture life without them. They'd made me a better man and I couldn't ask for more. I no longer had myself to live for because I had two little people looking up to me. I had to be the best example of a real man for my son and I had to show my daughter how a woman was supposed to be treated.

Chapter 35

Bam

What should have been the happiest day of my life has turned into the worst.

I was sitting up in my hospital bed while La'La laid beside me with her head on my chest. All I'd been doing was staring at the wall, listening to the beeps of the machines for the last two hours. I wanted to go home, but I allowed Alani to talk me into staying so that they could observe me overnight.

I'd denied all visits with the exception of my sister. As always, she had been the only one I could count on. As I sat and reflected on my life, Rock came to mind. When I needed him the most, he wasn't there and now here I was all alone again.

My son was mine and now I had nothing, and I didn't think I could forgive him. When I held Josiah Rocky Thomas Jr.'s lifeless body, I died right then and there. His umbilical cord was wrapped so tightly around his neck I couldn't remove it. I was getting weak and I was losing so much blood that the water in the Jacuzzi had turned crimson. I passed out in the tub with my son clutched in my arms.

If it wasn't for La'La, I would've drowned. All I remember was waking up, coughing up a storm, while a look a relief washed over my friend's

152

face. My reality quickly came rushing back and I knew that my baby was gone. I went fucking berserk and it took forever for La'La to calm me down. When the paramedics got there, they stabilized me and took me out of the house. I locked eyes with Rock and if looks could kill, everybody would be buying black dresses.

Lil' Rocky was the spitting image of his father and I didn't know if I could ever bear to look into his face again. For the longest time, I'd pushed everybody out and refused to let anyone in. I'd always suffered with my own demons in silence. He knew things about me that I hadn't told anyone, not even La'La, but there were also things that not even he knew.

Rock left me alone, knowing that it was very possible that I could need him.

*****

Whenever I had a lot of shit on my mind, I went to the trap to unwind and get my mind right. Khan had some lil niggas in here running shit, and they'd been on their shit. At the same time, you can never be too sure, so I didn't mind coming in here double and triple checking behind these niggas.

Thoughts of Lil Rocky had been plaguing my mind to the point where I couldn't sleep most nights. And when that happened, I hugged the block. One thing I could honestly say was that money had never

153

betrayed me. Money was always here for me whenever I needed it and had never turned its back on me.

Losing my son was the worst pain I'd ever experienced. I loved him before I ever even met him. The thing that pained me the most was that I didn't get to shower him with all the love a mother was supposed to give her child, all the love I never received from my mother.

Rocky never got a chance to see my face or feel the love I had for him. But I know that he is looking down on me and making sure I'm straight. We bonded over the time that I was carrying him. Every flutter he gave me, every time he kicked me in my ribs, every time he made me run to the bathroom, countless times throughout the day, and every time he made me teat everything in sight, he was making sure that he left me with plenty of fond memories to remember him by. He was well aware of the fact that his time with me was limited so he wanted to ensure we made the best of it. I know in my heart that God was short an angel and needed Rocky, but that didn't make it hurt any less.

After I finished up making my rounds to all the traps, I made my way home. As soon as I walked through the front door of my house, I broke down. I hadn't shed a tear since I was a little girl. I always told myself that I would never let anything else in this cold cruel world get me down.

154

But when I promised myself that all those years ago, I didn't know the pain of losing a child, a pain that I wouldn't wish on my worst enemy.

EllaSoul Productions

Chapter 36

Brooke

♫ I know you're tired of loving, of loving with nobody to love ♫

To my surprise, Khan had been an awesome father to KJ. He didn't miss a beat. I didn't have to call and ask him for anything when it came down to his son. I was more than happy that my son made it. I heard through the grapevine that Bam's demon seed died, and honestly, it served her right for almost killing mine.

It had been a great feeling to have Khan here with me and I was starting to feel as if my little family was complete. My six weeks were almost up and I no longer had to worry about little Miss La'La stepping back into the picture. She had herself a new man and even though I thought he was sexy as all get out, he ain't no Khan. I think that I was happier than she was to find out she was with someone else.

My life was finally falling into place. It's about time something worked out in Brooke's favor. For a while I was feeling like if it wasn't for bad luck, I'd have no luck at all. But as of late, things had been looking up for me. I had to get Khan out of my house so that I could set some shit up for tonight. I was about to put it on his ass something serious.

I'd picked up some really sexy shit and I was about to show him what he'd been missing out on all these years. I was going to cook him dinner and put it on his ass. I needed to solidify my spot in his life to make sure that he never strayed again. With me was where he belonged, and I was determined to show him just that.

When he made it back, I hit the radio allowing Pandora's Slow Jams station to fill the house. When he walked into the house, I walked to the door. I was standing there in nothing but my knock-off red bottoms and some lingerie I'd picked up from the flea market. Times were hard and I didn't have the luxury of Khan dropping off money for me to do as I pleased. I had to live modestly, but I was adjusting. If things went as planned, I wouldn't have to adjust for much longer.

He was looking good as fuck rocking a white and red Chasin' Faces outfit with a pair of white and red 23's on his feet. Chasin' Faces was a local up-and-coming clothing line started by local hood celebrity, Rae Hooks. His dreads were swinging, and his goatee was lined to perfection.

"What the fuck is all this shit for, Brooke?" He had the nerve to ask me with a smug look on his face.

"I cooked dinner for you and I wanted to show you how much I appreciate you," I replied with a smile still plastered across my face.

"Bitch, you look a fucking mess. All that makeup on your face got you looking like homie the clown. That swap meet lace shit you got on looks like it's about to give you a yeast infection, your red bottoms are orange, you can't cook so I'm not eating shit you prepared, and your fucking tracks is showing.

"Take this and go get your shit together," he growled slapping some money in my hands. "And you don't ever have to thank me for taking care of my son; that's my fucking job," he said heading towards the door.

"Where the fuck is he at anyway?" he asked me with pure disgust written all over his face.

"He's with your mother," I told him on the verge of tears. He'd completely crushed my spirits.

"I'm going to get him and he's going to be staying with me until I feel like bringing him back. Don't call my phone for shit 'cause I ain't got shit for you. I don't know why you thought you could ever be my bitch looking like that," he said and shook his head, walking out the door.

My tears started falling as I watched him walk out of the door and I didn't even bother to try and

158

wipe them off. I had something for that ass, though. This would be the last time he made a fool out of me.

EllaSoul Productions

Chapter 37

Khan

♫ I love things about her (but I don't love her) ♫

This bitch crazier than I thought if she had even an inkling of a thought that we were getting together. That hoe ain't nothing but my baby mama, that's it and that's all.

I'd been handling everything at all the traps since Alani left and Bam and Rock lost the baby. Bam had completely cut herself off from the world and not even Alani knew where she was. We knew she would be back, we just didn't know when.

On another note, my life had never been this hectic. I could possibly have three kids with three women, two of which had already been confirmed. I didn't need a DNA test for my daughter 'cause I knew that's she was mine, but I had to make sure KJ was mine before I did anything. I wanted Shaunda to get an invasive paternity test, but she flat out refused. That bitch better not be on no bullshit or I was going kick her ass.

I felt bad about how I'd been avoiding La'La, and even worse for the fact that I haven't seen my fucking seed behind it. I ain't even really get to hold my baby girl for real and I'd been fucked up about it. Neither one of them deserved it and I had to do better starting now. I had a trunk full of clothes, shoes, baby toys, baby food, the whole nine yards.

I got her address from my mother and I figured now was as good a time as any to get to know my baby girl. I grabbed a few bags from the trunk of my Infinity truck and made my way to her front door. Her new nigga's car wasn't out front, so I was hoping that his ass wasn't there so that I could also work on getting my wife back without his cock blocking ass being in my mix.

I went and knocked on the door and got a big, nasty shock. Here this nigga was opening the door with a pair of ball shorts and his shirt off, all sweaty like he just got finished working out. I frowned my face in disgust.

"Yo, where my wife at?" I asked him, getting pissed off.

"Bae, your punk ass, soon to be EX HUSBAND at the door," he said and walked away laughing.

Alani descended the stairs with nothing but a silk robe on. I now knew the reason behind his appearance… HE WAS FUCKING MY WIFE!

"What are you doing here, Khan, and how do you know where I live?" She asked, getting straight to the point.

"I want to see my fucking daughter. What the fuck you mean, 'why am I here?' You know what, just go get her so we can bond. I am her father after all, or am I?" I gave her questioning glare.

I didn't mean it, though. I would never question the paternity of my daughter, but I wanted her to feel as bad as I've been feeling. As soon as the words left my mouth, I wished that I could've eaten them.

"Rich let me talk to him alone for a minute. Go upstairs and check on Kay-Kay and I'll let you know when you can bring her down to see her 'DADDY'," she said putting emphasis on the word daddy. Rich slapped her ass as he walked past and then smirked at me.

He disappeared into the house and I'll never miss the menacing glare she gave me.

"Let's get something real clear so that there will be no more confusion. You are not fucking needed in my life, point blank period. You fucked up our relationship, not me, so how dare you bring your ass to my fucking place of residence and question the paternity of my fucking child, you stupid bitch?"

"I didn't mean it like that," I tried to defend myself.

162

"Shut the fuck up! I'm not done talking," she snapped with her eyes turning dark.

I'd never heard her talk, nor had I seen her get like this in all the years that we'd been together.

"Now I will never deny you the opportunity to see your child, nor will I bother to inquire as to why you've never even held her since she's been born. What I will say is…" she said walking up into my personal space, "…you ever, and I do mean ever, disrespect me again, and you'll be picking your lips up off of the fucking floor. And that's not a threat, it's a promise."

Rich came out and gave me my Karizma and I was completely smitten. She barely looked like me, though. It was as if La'La had spit her out. She did have my dimples and my eyes, though. I sat in the living room playing with my daughter and I was so happy that she immediately took to me. She must've known that her real daddy was here.

I made her a promise that I would never leave her again and I planned on keeping it.

Chapter 38

Rich

♫ Beauty is her name ♫

Now was as good a day as any to get my baby out of the house. We were child-free while Karizma was with her sperm donor. In all my years, I'd never disliked a nigga as much as I disliked him. You have to be a different type of coward to fuck over a good woman, and Alani is the epitome of a good woman. The way she takes care of Karizma you wouldn't even know that she's a new mother.

I could tell that thoughts of Khan had been plaguing her mind since his surprise visit. I didn't want to pressure her into anything, but she needed to go ahead and dead that marriage shit.

I understand the fact that they had history and what not, but we were building a future, it's just a plus that her pussy fits my dick like a glove. Once her six weeks were up, it was on and popping. I'd never come across a bitch whose pussy tasted as sweet as hers does.

Tonight, I was taking her to Ruth Chris because she just loves her steak, and it's not too far from the house.

"Bae, yo' ass still ain't ready yet?" I asked her, laughing.

We have reservations for eight o'clock and here it is seven forty-five and her ass still wasn't ready.

"I'm coming, nigga. You can't rush perfection," she said walking down the stairs looking like a bag of money. My growling stomach prevented me from jumping her bones right then and there.

La'La was decked out in a cream-colored Gucci dress with her back out and gold diamond incrusted Sergio Rossi Mermaid pumps. Those ran a nigga's pockets about $2,000, but I didn't care because my baby wanted them and they looked hella good on her feet. I didn't have a foot fetish, but I could damn sure suck on Alani's toes because her feet were just that pretty. She didn't have the type of toes that were run over; instead, they were nice and soft considering she got a pedicure every two weeks.

"Well, since you look that good all is forgiven," I said walking over and kissing her lips.

"Let's go baby, I'm hungry. And stop before you mess up my lipstick," she said pulling away and wiping my lips.

I couldn't help but to watch her ass as she walked away. Karizma had put a few pounds on her, but it was all right where it should be. Alani's ass had spread, and her hips looked fuller. Shit, like Red Man said, "it's just more cushion for the pushin".

165

We hopped inside of my Escalade truck and were out. I kept having this nagging feeling that something wasn't right, so I told La'La to call and check on Kay-Kay. Once she assured me that she was okay and that all was well, I could rest a little easier. But, I still felt as if something wasn't right. I shook the feeling off and continued to enjoy a night out with my lady. When we made it to the restaurant, we were quickly escorted to our seats.

We were having a great time just enjoying each other's company. Alani ordered a nine-ounce ribeye, medium well, with a loaded baked potato, and steamed broccoli. I had a porterhouse well done, with au gratin potatoes, and creamed spinach. I'm a hood nigga so I didn't really care for fancy steakhouses and shit, but my girl loved it. I needed my steak to be well done but she got hers medium well, claiming it was juicier that way. Then, for desert we shared a crème brulee.

When we left the steakhouse, we decided we weren't ready to go home so we went for a walk down the strip. While we were waiting for the valet to bring the car around, I watched my entire life flash before my eyes. One moment we were smiling and laughing in each other's faces, the next I was pushing her down on the ground and pulling out my Glock to bust back at whoever thought they were bold enough to shoot at me and my baby. It wasn't anything but the grace of God that we didn't have Kay with us.

166

Whoever it was wasn't even smart enough to wait and ensure they could hit their intended targets but did it in front of a crowded restaurant. When I was sure the coast was clear, I went to check on my baby since I'd pushed her to the ground and I was grief-stricken. La'La's cream colored dress was the shade of vermilion. Her body was twisted at an odd angle, and she wasn't moving. What the fuck could happen next?!

Chapter 39

Shaunda

♫ How the hell can we be lovers if we don't even love each other ♫

I laid back on this cold, hard steel table and thought of all the decisions I'd made in life this far. I thought I wanted Khan, but he'd put me on the back burner for his "wife". To make matters worse, he'd been around Brooke's loose pussy ass. So, here I was with my legs spread eagle about to get an abortion because I refused to keep coming second in his life, or third, fourth, and fifth for that matter.

I knew he was going to be mad at me for this, but fuck it, he needed to tighten up. That's not the only reason I was getting rid of this baby; I didn't even know if it was his, but that's neither here nor there. He'd never know that, though. Tears slid from the corners of my eyes and onto the steel slab as I felt them suction my unborn child out of me. Even if I wanted to back out, it was too late for that now.

*****

When I got to my loft, I wanted nothing more than to lay in bed and sleep. Walking into my room, I got the shock of my life. There laid a shirtless Khan in the middle of my bed. The absolute last person I expected to see was him after I'd just murdered what could have possibly been his baby.

168

But I couldn't deny how good he looked. Without even moving, the muscles in his back flexed, causing my pussy to jump, but the large maxi pad that doubled as a damn diaper in between my legs told me that I couldn't act off of the way that my body was feeling.

"Where you been?" he asked with his back still facing me.

I didn't even know that he was up. But then again, I never had been able to creep up on him.

"I was ummm… at my mother's house," I said reciting the first lie that came to my head.

"You don't even like your mother so I'mma give a couple of minutes while you fix me something to eat to come up with a better lie," he stated, getting up and walking into my bathroom. I used that as my opportunity to do exactly what he said. I don't even know why I'd said I was at my mother's house when I hadn't talked to her ass in years.

I took out some boneless, skinless chicken breasts, fresh broccoli, and fettuccine pasta to make him some chicken alfredo. I preheated the oven to make the garlic bread and prepared a side Caesar salad. If there was one thing I could do, it was burn in the kitchen. I was prepared to do anything to keep him from finding out about my bleeding pussy when I'm supposed to be pregnant.

169

Just as I was about to drop the pasta in to the boiling hot water, I felt a sting on the side of my face as I fell to the floor. If I had to compare the pain to anything, it would be like a thousand bee and wasp stings. I looked up into Khan's eyes and there were flames dancing around in them.

"I'm going to ask you one more time," he said and paused to grab the collar of my shirt, "Where the fuck were you?" He asked me in a venom laced voice.

"I was out shopping," I said, saying the first thing that came to my head.

Smack!

"Bitch, lie again! If you were shopping, where the fuck is the bags?" he asked, still holding onto me with a death grip. "I didn't see anything that I liked," I told him, hoping my lie worked.

"Well what the fuck is this then?" He asked me with the papers from my abortion clutched tightly in his hand.

I cursed myself because I was caught red-handed. If I'd known he would be here, I would've thrown that shit away.

"Oh, so now you have nothing to say," he said tightening the grip he had on me.

I swallowed hard, not knowing what was on store for me.

"And here I was about to try and build something with your simple ass, but you go and kill my seed. All I want to know is why?" Khan said, searching my face for answers.

"You put me on the back burner, Khan! What the fuck was I supposed to do? Sit around and wait for you to get over your baby mama while me and my child go without? Get the fuck out of here with that bull shit!" I screamed, appalled by how selfish he was being.

"Fuck that shit you talking. You know I would've been there for my shorty, so you can miss me with that bullshit. I take care of all my kids," he countered loosening up his grip slightly.

"Fuck you, Khan! Fuck you, your bitch of a wife, and your fucking kids!" I yelled in his face while trying to push him off me. As soon as the words left my mouth, they tasted like ass.

I must've hit a nerve because he started beating my ass. I tried to go blow for blow with him, but I was still weak from the abortion. Not that I would've stood a chance against him anyway. I swear I could feel my lip bust, my cheek swell, and some blood vessels burst in my eye. He was hitting me like I was a random ass nigga on the streets. He beat me like I stole something.

171

Eventually, my fight or flight instincts kicked in and I tried to run away when I saw that he was getting tired. But then he grabbed me by my twenty-six inch sew-in and flung me into the stove. I flew head first into the oven, causing the glass to break and stick into various parts of my face. Khan looked like a mad man coming towards me. Afraid that he could possibly be about to kill me, I grabbed the pot of boiling water off the stove and threw it in his face.

"Bitch I'mma kill you when I get my hands on you," he screamed. I took that as my cue to run out of the house.

I could hear him shouting obscenities at me as I ran out the house and hopped into my car. I had no clue where I was going, the only thing I knew was that I had to get away from him.

EllaSoul Productions

Chapter 40

Bam

♫ And I might be crazyyyy, but you made me crazy ♫

I awoke from my sleep with a pain in my chest. I'd been having sleepless nights since the loss of my son, but the one night that I'd actually been able to go to sleep peacefully, I was awakened with the feeling that something was wrong. I could give less than a fuck if something happened to Rock, but my sister was a completely different story.

I reached over to grab my phone and before I could dial Alani's number, Rich was calling me.

"Bam, it's La'La. She got hit up."

Without bothering to offer him a reply, I hung up the phone. If I lost my bitch, I was sure to lose the last bit of sanity I had left.

I got to the hospital in record time and found Rich in the waiting room looking as if he had the weight of the world on his shoulders. I didn't really fuck with him at first, but eventually he grew on me. I couldn't do shit but respect the way he treated my girl. He really won me over with the way he treated my god daughter/niece. If you didn't know them personally, you could swear that he was Baby Kay's biological father.

173

"Yo, what happened?" I asked him.

His eyes were bloodshot and it was then I noticed that he was covered in blood. When our eyes met, I felt his pain. I knew that he genuinely loved La'La. Before he could answer, I heard Mama Megan.

"Bam, what are you doing here? Did you come to check on Khan?" She asked. She couldn't see Rich sitting in front of me from where she was standing. I turned to meet her eyes and she saw Rich sitting there.

"WHAT THE FUCK ARE YOU DOING HERE?" She screamed, drawing the attention of everybody that sat in the waiting room.

"Bitch, you better back the fuck up out my face. This is not the time," Rich said, standing up.

"Who you think you calling a bitch?" Megan's ass asked Rich, ready to turn up.

Usually, I was the one in the middle of everything, but I was actually trying to diffuse the situation this time.

"Yo, y'all need to chill the fuck out!" I yelled at the both of them.

"You need to be telling him that. He's the one being disrespectful," she stated in her defense, crossing her arms like a defiant child.

174

"What's going on over here?" I turned around and met eyes with Khan and Rock. Just when I thought my day couldn't get any worse.

"He called me a bitch!" Megan yelled to Khan like she was happy about telling her older brother about somebody picking on her at school.

"Yo, you disrespecting my moms, son?" Khan asked Rich getting more and more pissed off by the minute.

Those niggas already didn't like each other so all they needed was a reason to act out. It was then that I noticed Khan had bandages wrapped around the upper part of his torso, and his neck and parts of his face were red and swollen.

"Man, fuck you and that bitch," Rich snapped and the whole waiting room erupted in pure pandemonium. Megan, Khan, and Rock were fucking Rich up, although he was giving them a run for their money. Just as I was about to intervene like a night hawk, in swooped the sexiest man I'd ever seen in all my years.

He started swinging on everybody except Megan and Rich. He had his shirt off and every time he moved, the muscles flexed in his back making my nipples harden and my pussy throb. His skin was the perfect shade of espresso and his body stature was stocky, but not fat. His body was cut the fuck up.

175

Snapping out of my day dream, I snapped on everybody.

"Y'all dumb asses need to chill the fuck out! My motherfucking sister in here shot the fuck up, I don't even know what wrong with her, and y'all in here tripping."

As soon as the words left my mouth, it was like everybody stopped what they were doing. It was then they all noticed the dried blood covering Rich's hands, face, and clothes. Once the realization set in of what Rich and I were really here for, Megan fell out on the floor and Khan started kicking chairs and knocking over everything in his path. Before we could get to the bottom of what was wrong, the Doctor came out.

"Family of Alani Thomas," she asked with her clipboard in hand, scanning her eyes across the dismantled waiting room. We all rushed over to where she was standing.

"How are you all doing? I wish we could've all met under different circumstances, but here we are. My name is Dr. Bushwick. First things first, Alani is a solider and she's determined to live. She's flat lined twice and each time we were able to revive her. She was hit in the shoulder, which we've removed successfully… but she was also hit twice in the abdomen. We were able to remove them both also, but one ruptured her spleen and caused her to

EllaSoul Productions

lose the baby. We were able to repair everything but it's going to take some time for her to heal. She lost a lot of blood so she's going to need her rest. You can go back and see her, but not for long," she walked away as quickly as she came.

I turned to Rich just in time to see him walking away with my new boo hot on his trail. I knew he was going through it, and to know that your first child had been taken away from you too soon before you even knew they existed. I'd lost a child and that's a pain that I wouldn't wish on my worst enemy. Well, with the exception of the person who tried to kill my sister.

Khan was holding up a hysterical Megan and Rock came over trying to hold me. I tried to resist but he refused to let me go. Soon after, I just melted into his embrace. It just felt so right in his arms. I felt at home, safe, and secure all over again. I took a deep breath, inhaling his Creed Cologne, and fell in love all over again.

But that was all short lived.

"JOSIAH!" I heard some bitch yell from behind me. I turned and locked eyes with some tall, light-skinned, model thin bitch.

"Josiah, who the fuck is this?" She asked while pointing in my direction.

"Margo what the fuck you doing up here?" Rock asked her, and I could see that his jaw was clenched.

"My baby daddy didn't answer his phone when I called so I tracked it, and boom, here I am," she said. It was then that I noticed her protruding belly.

"Take your dumb ass home, Margo!" Rock growled.

"Not until you tell me who she is and what you're doing here," she said to him while placing her hand on her thin hip.

I was no longer paying them any attention, nor could I hear a thing they were discussing. When she said, "baby daddy", it felt as if I'd died on the inside. My breathing became labored and I felt faint. How could the one I gave my heart to do me like that?

"Is she your little sister?" The bitch I now knew as Margo asked him.

That was all it took. I jumped up and smacked the shit out of him.

"You're going to wish you never met me," I said to him and walked away. I had to go check on my sister.

EllaSoul Productions

Chapter 41

Rich

My head was all fucked up right now. My bitch laid up in a fucking hospital and then I have to go through the pain of knowing she was going to give birth to my seed, only to have him or her snatched away from me. I couldn't stay in that fucking hospital.

It might seem as if I didn't care, but that's not the case at all. I care too much, and I couldn't take seeing my baby girl connected to all those fucking machines and shit. I was fucking shit up my entire way out of the hospital.

"Chill the fuck out my nigga, them peoples coming," my homie Blake said, referring to twelve of the boys in blue coming our way.

I met Blake back when I was twelve and he was thirteen. My mother, Robyn, was a sociopath and she was in an insane asylum for killing my father. Once she was sentenced to spend the rest for her years in the fucking nut house, Blake's mother, Brenda, took me in. Three years later, she died of breast cancer. Being that he never knew his father, we were on our own.

It'd been us against the world ever since. We used to hustle small time so that we could eat, keep the bills up on Blake's Mama's house, and pay for

EllaSoul Productions

studio time. See, hustling was what we did to survive, but we always had bigger aspirations on getting the fuck out of the hood. All we did was fuck bitches, trap, and rap.

While on the block, we would always spit shit to each other and we would also write our shit down. We believed in ourselves enough knowing that we would make it one day.

"I'm going to have to ask you guys to leave. We've gotten several calls about disturbances," one of the cops said.

"It's cool, pimp, I got 'em," Blake said leading me out of the hospital. I was going to paint the city red looking for whoever it was that destroyed my fucking life.

Chapter 44

Rock

The look on Sophie's face when Margo walked in tore through my soul. I felt like shit immediately. There was not a day that went by that I didn't think about her and my son. I wondered who he would have looked more like, me or Bam.

"Who was that bitch?" Margo asked me once Bam was out of earshot.

"None of your fucking business," I told her, rubbing my temples, trying to calm down.

"Umm, I'm five months pregnant with your child. I think somebody hugging up on my man is my fucking business," she indignantly stated with her hands perched perfectly on her small hips.

"Don't ask me for the answer to a question that you ain't ready to hear. Now take your dumb ass home," I told her pushing her gently towards the exit.

I now knew the chances of me getting my girl back were slim to none. I scooped up Khan and we made our way back to go see what was up with my sister.

I never meant to hurt Bam, shit just seemed to happen that way. Nobody ever wanted to admit it, but women could actually push their man into the arms of another woman. Bam would start tripping out on me whenever she got good and ready to do so. When I wasn't stepping out on her, she would do some dumb ass shit like poison a nigga's food if I wasn't home when she wanted me to be. She acted like she didn't already know that the business came with late nights and early mornings.

If she was a green bitch to the lifestyle, I could understand, but Bam busted her guns alongside me so she knew how this shit went. However, she made me pay for mistakes that I hadn't even committed yet. I wanted Bam back, but I'm a boss ass nigga that was not going to beg her little ass for a spot back inside of her life.

I'm a man who was far from perfect, so Bam would have to just accept me as a work in progress. I could try to do better, but she would have to try as well. As long as I had put up with her foolishness, she could stand to put up with my shit for a little bit.

Chapter 42

Alani

♫ Set the world on fire! ♫

I woke up confused about where I was. I tried to sit up and it felt as if someone had sat a brick on my stomach. I tried to move my arm and a pain shot through me. My right arm was in a sling, so I moved my left arm to touch my stomach and it was wrapped in bandages. I was in so much pain and my body felt tremendously weak.

It was then that everything came rushing back to me. Starting with me going out to dinner with Rich and ending with me getting popped three times. Everything happened so fast that I didn't even get a chance to bust back. Just as I was about to push the button to call the nurse's station, in walked my best bitch.

"How you feeling, sis?" Bam asked, walking over to my hospital bed.

She looked so stressed that it was written all over her face. She could try to cover that shit up with everybody else, but not me.

"I'll live, but what's up with you?" I asked her, filled with concern.

"Nothing you need to worry your pretty little head about. What we need to be worried about is

184

getting at whomever deemed it necessary to wet you up," she said with her eyes growing dark and cold.

That's the thing with Bam, she was always and forever the perfect shoulder to lean on and vent to about your problems. But when it came time to share her own, she was extremely tight-lipped.

I knew something was up with my sister, I just wished she would let me in sometimes. I wanted to be there for her like she was for me. I couldn't ask for a better friend and confidant than the one that I had in Bam. I just knew something was troubling her and I wanted to help her though it, but I couldn't do that if she wouldn't tell me what's up.

"I don't even know who it is, but when I find out, that bitch is going to feel me," I said with the wheels turning in my head.

"Do you at least have a clue who it is?" she asked me with questioning eyes.

"Time will reveal all," I told her, leaning back in bed.

I had a feeling it was Brooke's bitter ass that shot me. Her ditzy ass didn't even have the smarts to grab another car. I knew that raggedy ass Honda from anywhere and she didn't even have it tinted. I was going to make that bitch die a slow and painful death for this shit. I didn't even want Khan's community dick ass no more and that bitch still

185

wanted to fuck with me. I guess she wanted me completely out of the picture. That hoe must know that there were no wins with me, so she wanted to completely wipe me out.

Her time were coming, and I'd be her judge, jury, and executioner.

Bam had crawled in the bed with me and I just rubbed her head as I always did when we were in our feelings. The doctor walked in with a smile on her face.

"I see that you're up. How are you feeling?" she asked me. I just looked at her without bothering to reply. I'd just been shot; how did she think I was feeling?

"Well I'll go and get the nurse to bring you something for the pain. The good news is you'll make a full recovery but being that you were shot in the abdomen we weren't able to save the baby."

I completely zoned out after that, nothing else she said registered in my head. Hearing that I was knocked up and didn't know it upset me. But being as though I would never get to see or hold my child, crushed me, all because a hating ass bitch didn't like me over a nigga that loved me. I didn't regret being with or meeting Khan because I wouldn't have my daughter, and Karizma is my life. I just hated the fact that all my problems were surrounding him. I had plans to make Brooke hurt,

186

and she was going to regret ever trying to get one over on a bitch like me.

EllaSoul Productions

Chapter 43

Khan

♫ I gotta live with the fact I did you wrong forever ♫

Shaunda got me fucked all the way up. If she thought I beat her ass the first time, she had another thing coming. When I got my hands on that bitch, I had plans to strangle her ass. I managed to call Rock, then my mother, and went to the hospital. My entire body was on fire from Shaun throwing that boiling hot water on my ass. Good thing none of it really hit me in my face, only my neck and torso. I didn't know where Shaunda's ass went, but she hauled ass. I didn't even mean to put my hands on her, but she straight up lied to my face like I was some poo-poo ass nigga.

If I hadn't found those papers from the abortion clinic, she probably wouldn't ever have told me that she'd killed my seed. Then, she had the nerve to talk shit about my wife and other kids. That shit just caused me to snap. My mother always instilled in me to never hit women and in Khanna to never let a nigga hit her, but fuck that. I don't hit women, but I'll smack a bitch.

I walked towards Alani's hospital room feeling like the world was closing in on me. Somebody actually had balls enough to touch my baby. We'd run the entire 757 for as long as I could

188

remember so everybody knew my wife was off limits. She's more than just the mother of my child, she was my business partner.

She hadn't really been out in the field since we broke up, and on top of that, she'd just had Karizma... but she was still in the know about everything that went on. I just needed to get her back. Shit was never the same when you were missing your rib.

I walked into her room and she was lying in bed with Bam. A once strong woman looked weak and broken. Bam looked over at me, got up, and walked out of the room. I was glad she did because I wanted to talk to La'La alone.

"How you feeling, baby girl?" I asked her, sitting on the edge of her bed.

She just sat there staring blankly into space. I took her foot into my hand and started rubbing it. She looked so stressed, but eventually I could see the relaxation set into her face. After about five minutes of silence, she asked me, "What do you want from me, Khan?"

I didn't even have to think of an answer to her question.

"I want you. I'm sick of living without you. You're the air that I breathe and I'm suffocating without you. I've been off my square since you've

189

been gone and I want you back. Scratch that, I need you back. I want my family all under one roof and we can't do that having Kay-Kay going back and forth from house to house. Plus, I don't want another nigga around my kid," I told her in all seriousness.

"You fucked up what we had, not me and now you mad because a nigga stepping up to the plate to do what you couldn't and wouldn't? Karizma didn't even see you for the first couple of weeks of her life. Now you want to waltz your ass in here like some father and husband of the year? Our entire marriage is a sham. We haven't even been together since we got married. A day that was supposed to be special to me was ruined because of selfish decisions that you made. You've hurt me so much, Khan. Every time I look at you, I relive all the dog shit you've done to me. With Rich, I don't have to question; I always felt safe with him. On top of all that, where does your son and your new baby fit into this equation?" She stated with a smug look adorning her face.

"He fits in with us. I don't want his mother, and this is a known fact. Plus, I don't have another baby," I told her feeling a little sad that Shaunda had killed my baby. "And you feel safe with him, but you were with him when you got wet up. He must not have been doing so great of a job at protecting you," I said feeling salty as fuck. I didn't care if I sounded like a punk or not.

190

"AGAIN, I HAVE SUFFERED BECAUSE OF YOU! Your bitch shot me! We're not even together and that bitch still feels threatened by me," she screamed with tears streaming down her face.

That shit fucked me all up. My mother always taught me that if you made your girl cry then you were less than a man. I had to be a certified bitch because all I'd ever made La'La do was cry. I just kissed her forehead and left her room. The last thing I ever wanted to do was cause her any pain. Since I had already, I refused to bring her any more. If that meant we had no relationship outside of co-parenting, then so be it. I guess I just had to live with the consequences of my selfish decisions.

The thing that fucked me up the most was her saying my bitch had shot her. It couldn't have been Shaunda because the bitch was too busy killing my baby and throwing boiling hot water in my face.

Chapter 44

Bam

After leaving Alani's hospital room, I stayed back to watch Rock. When he left the hospital, I followed him to a small, middle-class neighborhood in the heart of Norfolk. I parked a few houses down and watched him park in the drive way of a modest-sized white house with a blue trim. I waited until all the lights in the house were off before I hopped out of my car and made my way toward the house.

Making my way around to the back of the house, I picked the lock and went inside. I checked all the rooms down stairs and once I ensured they were all empty, I made my way toward the stairs. When I made it to the top of the stairs, I noticed a room with the light from the TV illuminating the hallway. I decided to check that room last.

The first room that I checked was empty, but the second murdered my spirit. It was a nursery painted blue, black, and white. I stepped further into the room and stopped in front of the blown-up poster-sized photo a 3D-ultrasound. As I stared at the photo, my heart started to ache for my son. There was his name clear as day for me to see: Josiah Rocky Thomas, Jr.

How could they take my son's name like that? They were trying to replace him and there was no way I could let that happen. I was tempted to

192

back out and leave the house the way I came in, but I convinced myself that they had to feel my pain.

After ensuring the entire house was empty with the exception of the room with the TV on, I went further inside. The way the bedroom was set up, there was a wall blocking the door so I was able to peek around the wall and get a full view of the entire room except for the master bathroom. My heart was not prepared for the sight before me.

"Damn! Baby throw that ass back. Oh shit just like that," grunted a naked Rock.

"Oh shit baby I'm about to cum," Margo moaned out.

I knew it was her from her reflection in the mirror in the head board, not to mention the protruding belly.

"Go ahead baby, I'm right behind you," Rock encouraged her.

Everybody tried to make me out to be this evil bitch, but at least I was nice enough to let them get their rocks off first.

"Well, well, well what do we have here?" I said, now making my presence known. They had me tickled pink, as I watched them scramble to cover themselves.

EllaSoul Productions

"Rock I don't know what you're trying to cover yourself up, for I've already seen all that," I snickered.

"Bam what the fuck are you doing?" He had the nerve to ask me.

"I came to have some fun with y'all," I stated matter-of-factly, stepping further into the room. His little bitch was screaming and crying her head off. "Bitch, shut the fuck up! Don't you see me trying to have a conversation with my baby daddy?" I snapped.

It didn't help because she kept screaming.

POW!

I shot the bitch in her foot. I knew that was going to make her keep screaming, but at least now she has a reason to.

"Sophie, come on man! She's pregnant, yo – chill the fuck out!" Rock growled getting out of the bed and coming in my direction. His dick was swinging back and forth, reminding my kitty of what I'd been missing out on.

"Your ass didn't care that fucking much when I was pregnant with our son. Then you have the nerve to try and give that bitch's baby my son's name?" I told him, trying to remain stone faced.

194

"What is she talking about Josiah?" Margo asked him, wrapping the sheet around her foot.

I guess the only thing that caught her attention was talk of my son.

"Bitch, I'm not ready for you yet. When I get finished talking to my baby daddy, I'll let you know," I screamed at her then turned back to Rock.

His long dick continued to swing from side to side slapping his thighs slightly with each step he took. I had to make myself snap back to the matter at hand and make my mouth stop watering.

"Baby Daddy? Who is this bitch, Josiah?" Margo asked him again.

"Bitch ask one more fucking question. I told you I wasn't ready for you yet so shut the fuck up!" I yelled, leaped on the bed, and began pistol whipping her anywhere my hands landed.

"Bam, stop!" I felt arms wrap around me.

"Fuck you, Rock! You were laid up with this bitch while our son was dying. I almost died. I called you and you weren't there. I needed you and you left me. Why couldn't you just love me, Mommy? Why did you let all those things happen to me, Mommy?" I cried.

"Shh, it's okay baby girl," my mother whispered into my hair.

195

"No, it's not mommy. I have nobody now. Rock wasn't there for me and he let my baby die. Why did he lie to me, Mommy? He said he would always be there for me."

"I'm still here," I heard Rock's voice say snapping me out of my trance.

"I'm going to make sure I'm the last person you hurt," I said, grabbing the combat knife that was strapped to my thigh and jabbing it in his hand. He let me go and I dived back on the bed, stabbing his bitch in the stomach hopefully killing her and his love child. I almost died, and my son did die, so I could give less than a fuck about her and her son.

I found out through the grapevine that the day I went into labor with lil' Rocky he was laid up with this hoe. I just didn't know who she was at that point in time. He tackled me just as I was about to stab her again and we tussled over the knife. He eventually got the knife out of my hand, but I grabbed my .357 out of my boots. When he noticed that I had it he tried to get it out of my hands and it went off. I don't know where he got hit but once he rolled off of me I whispered in his ear, "Hell has no fury like a woman scorned. See you in hell, Rock."

I straightened out my clothes and walked towards the door.

"Oh, and for the record the love that I had, well still have for you is real. But I told myself that

196

anybody that deems it necessary to hurt me has to pay. You are just a casualty of war."

On my way, I cut the gas burners on and lit a match. I didn't want there to be a trace of the people who played a part in ruining my life. At least that's what I'd convinced myself.

EllaSoul Productions

Chapter 45

Alani

Recovering and trying to take care of an infant was next to impossible. Rich and Khan had been out searching the city for who shot me because I wouldn't tell them who I thought it was. Mark my words though, when I catch up to that hoe, it's over with for her ass.

With my one good arm, I carried Karizma's car seat to my car and did my best at strapping her in. It took me about five minutes, but I eventually got her secured and was one my way. When I pulled up to my attorney's office, I grabbed my baby, her diaper bag, and my Tory Burch hand bag. I walked inside and to the front desk.

"I'm here to see Mrs. Fitz," I told the receptionist.

"I'll let her know you're here. Just have a seat in the waiting area and I'm sure she'll be out here shortly," she smiled and told me while picking up the phone to page her.

I sighed but went to go sit in the waiting area for her.

"Mrs. Thomas," I heard a woman say as soon as I got comfortable and soothed a fussy Karizma.

EllaSoul Productions

"You can just call me Alani," I said, standing up and sitting Karizma's carrier down to shake her hand.

"Well, Alani come right this way and we can get started," Mrs. Fitz said while she led the way to her office.

"Let me help you with some of that," she said grabbing Karizma's baby carrier from me. For that, I was very grateful because that was the heaviest thing that I had in my hands. She had gotten so fat over the months it was crazy. Sometimes I just held her and looked into her eyes. I never knew what real love felt like until I had her.

I know that I may not be perfect, but I knew she loved me despite all of my flaws. She didn't care if I had my face full of makeup, if I chose to wear sweats that day, or if I was draped in the finest jewels. She's just happy that I was there.

"Thank you so much, she is killing my arm," I said, following her into the office.

Stepping in, I took a moment to admire her décor. She had a spacious office with huge floor to ceiling bay windows overlooking Virginia Beach, a solid red oak desk, with plush Morella black ice wall-to-wall carpet. In the far corner of the office, and a small wet bar with Aksehir Siyahi marble. In the center of the room sat a black Italian leather sectional with Red accent pillows.

199

"Thank you, I decorated myself," she said, taking notice to me admiring her office. She took a seat behind her desk and removed a crying Karizma from carrier.

"I'll take her," I said sitting my bags down on the sectional.

"Girl please, I got her," she said, soothing her. "So, let's get down to business," Mrs. Fitz stated, cradling Kay-Kay with one arm and opening a file with the other.

"Well, it looks like you guys own a few properties together," she said, skimming the file. "I don't care. He can have all that shit. I just need to rid myself of him. Most of my life's problems come from him so I don't want to have any dealings with him outside of that little girl right there," I responded pointing at my daughter.

She adjusted her Giorgio Armani thin wire-framed specks and cleared her throat. She looked to be in her mid-twenties, but the barely noticeable small patches of salt and peppered hair around the temples of her asymmetric hi-low bob said otherwise. She was a very beautiful woman with smooth skin the color of cocoa and not a wrinkle in sight. Her stacked frame was decked out in all-black Ted Baker Dardee embellished midi-dress and black Alexander McQueen embroidered peep-toe pumps.

200

Her cheek bones where high and well-defined, accentuating her face. She had a lightly dusted purple eye shadow, her lips were full and pouty, painted purple just like her nails, and I noticed a purple Celine bag sitting over in the corner.

"Before we attempt to go any further, let me say this. People will only do what you allow them to do. So with that being said, I want you to know your worth from here on out, baby girl. You're too beautiful to let someone walk all over you, and I'm pretty sure you have your pick of the litter when it comes to getting men."

I let everything that she said marinate in my mind for a second. I usually got mad when someone tried to tell me something about my relationSHIT with Khan, but for some odd reason, I welcomed her wise words. I'd loved Khan from the deepest pits of my soul for almost as long as I'd known him, yet he had shitted on me time and time again. Even though I was with Rich now, Khan still had a hold on me, and it was now time for me to regain my power, starting with this divorce.

"Tell me something I don't know," I told her sighing.

"I know how you are feeling, but it's okay. I'm pretty sure I can get this annulled. If not, I'll try to make the official divorce as speedy as possible."

I would be forever grateful for her, especially since she had calmed Karizma's colicky behind. It seemed like the only people that could get and keep her under wraps were Rich, her father, Megan, my mother, and Khanna. I guess I could add my lawyer, Mrs. Fitz, to that list.

I signed all the necessary paperwork to have Khan served with our divorce papers. To all his little side hoes it might seem like they were winning, but in the end, I would emerge victorious. They could have him, the infidelity, the STD's, the outside children, and all that good shit. I just hoped that he was man enough to allow this process to be quick and painless.

I started to gather my things to make my departure.

"Girl you have to let me keep this fat baby sometimes. She is a joy to have around," she said cradling Kay-Kay and following me out of the door.

"Sure, I see no problem with that. It gets so overwhelming sometimes to the point where I want to pull my hair out," I told her laughing "I really appreciate all this, Mrs. Fitz," I told her sincerely.

"Well, part of it is my job. The other half I have no problem with. I love children even though I have none of my own," she said with a faraway look in her eyes "And when it comes to relationships, I've been there, done that, and got the t-shirt."

She walked me all the way to my car and even stopped to strap Karizma in.

"Thank you so much, Mrs. Fitz! I am forever indebted to you," I gushed.

"Child please, call me Markita."

"Okay Markita, thanks again," I said hugging her.

Once I saw her walk back into her office, I pulled off. It was time to start a new phase in my life. Khan would be nothing in my life except a father to Karizma and even that was contingent on whether he wanted to be or not. I would never beg him to be in his child's life. That decision was completely up to him.

EllaSoul Productions

Chapter 46

Rich

I'd gone crazy trying to find out who it was that touched my wife and the fact that she wouldn't tell me shit had been blowing me. I'd ridden the entire seven cities alongside my nigga Blake and put money out there for anybody who could bring me any information or point me in the right direction.

Between looking for this mystery person and burning up tracks in the studio, I hadn't really spent any time with my baby. But I was going to make that shit all the way up to her.

I stopped by Agent Provocateur and picked her up a Black and nude bra, thong, and suspender set. That shit ran me 'bout $2,300, but Alani was worth it. I grabbed her some nude Giuseppe Zanotti's and paid for Diamond and her crew to give her the works. I picked up a ton of other shit for her too, just because.

I didn't want Alani to have to lift a finger, so I took Karizma to her mother's house. Alani's mother was the sweetest person in the world, that was, until you get on her bad side. She took to me immediately, but that didn't stop her from asking me twenty-one questions or pulling out her gun and threating me if I hurt her daughter. I guess that's where La'La got that thug shit from.

When I got back to the house, I laid what I wanted her to wear out for her and went down to the kitchen. I already had two T-bone steaks thawed out and marinated. All I needed to do was turn on our outside barbeque so that I could grill them. I made a side salad, garlic-chive mashed potatoes, and fresh greens beans.

La'La didn't have a clue of the fact that I could burn in the kitchen just as well as her ass, if not better. After I finished cooking, I placed everything inside of the warmer so that I could prepare the house for Alani's arrival.

I placed rose petals around the house leading to the master bathroom and placed some inside of the tub in her bathwater. When she made it home, I watched her from the cameras in my man cave. I got mad all over again seeing her arm still in a sling, but instantly perked up seeing her gorgeous face. I watched her bend over to pick up the card that laid in front of the door.

She read it then smiled the card had read:

Each day that I get to wake up to your beautiful face makes that day worth living. I promise to spend my life righting all his wrongs, so you'll never have to hurt again. I love you, Alani Clarke!

She then followed the rose petals to the bathroom. I watched as she picked up the single long-stemmed rose that sat beside a glass of champagne on top of another card. She sniffed the rose before picking up the next card to read that one as well.

> *You've have been through so much in your short life and I think it's time for you to sit back and relax. I want you to soak in the Jacuzzi that I have already filled with one of your favorite bubble baths from bath and body works, Forever Red. Don't worry, I'll send for you when it's time for the next phase of your night.*

She then stripped out of her jogging suit by PINK and it took everything in my power to not go in there slide right up in her gushy. Her ass sat up so perfectly if I didn't know any better I would swear that she paid to get her booty like that. Alani's ass was the only place on her body that had stretch marks. Not that I minded because if a bitch's booty ain't got stretch marks then I think it's childish. But my baby's booty was full grown; that just let me know she'd earned her stripes.

I took notice to how she cradled her arm closely to her frame once the sling was off. The person that hurt her was going to pay dearly with their life. Every day that I had to watch her not be able to use her arm to its full potential a fire started

EllaSoul Productions

to brew inside of me. Every day that I had to hear her cry because she wasn't able to do certain things with Karizma that she usually did, it angered me more. I still didn't know why somebody would want to hurt my baby.

Alani was the sweetest person I had ever crossed paths with… well, except if you cross her or her family. She didn't even really have enemies with the exception Brooke. She was the only person that I could imagine hating her enough. But at the same time, I couldn't picture Brooke suiting up and riding out to shoot somebody. Every day I had to rack my brain and try to figure out who would want to take my baby girl out.

Snapping back to the task at hand, I looked back at the camera and watched Alani as she wrapped her hair up, step into the Jacuzzi tub, and take a sip of her champagne before leaning her head back on the bath pillow. A smile crept onto my face watching her actually get a chance to relax for a change. She was always ripping and running around, making sure that everybody and everything else was straight, never taking time for herself. She was usually so consumed with her family's matters and being a mother that she never got a chance to just unwind and relax. But as her man, that was where I came in.

While she was in the tub, I took a quick shower in my man cave and went down to the kitchen to ensure everything was set up correctly. When I made it back inside of my man cave, I noticed she was no longer in the tub or in the bathroom at all for that matter.

I looked between each camera and saw that she had gone into our bedroom and changed into the lingerie that I'd purchased for her earlier. Instead of putting on the thong, she laid back in the bed and began playing in her pussy. Alani had the prettiest, pinkest pussy I had ever seen on a bitch, and believe me, I'd had a plethora of pussy thrown my way. Her pussy just sat up just right, her lips didn't sag or have all that extra skin sagging all around it, and her pretty clit sat up and out just right. She dipped her fingers inside of her honey pot then circled them around her clit. She brought her hand up to her mouth to taste herself then went right back in. She brought herself to a small orgasm before getting out of the bed and going into her walk-in closet.

La'La came out with what looked like a small treasure chest. After opening it, she looked around inside it for a few seconds; I guess she found what she was looking for because she then skipped back to the bed.

She laid back and it was then that I was able to get a good look at what she had. Alani had grabbed some anal beads, a rabbit, and a bullet. I didn't even know that she had all that, but I was

208

going to sit back and enjoy the show she was putting on for a nigga.

She eased three of the five anal beads into her ass as she sucked on the rabbit lubricating it. For her arm to have still needed to use a sling, she sure was working with it. Then, she placed the bullet on her clit and the rabbit inside her pussy and started going to town.

She was biting down on her bottom lip as an orgasm took over her body. When she pulled the rabbit out, she squirted out all over the bed. I swear that some of it hit the throw rug in front of our bed. When she went back in, it wasn't too long before she was squirting again.

I just sat back, watching her at first, but then she looked into the camera and looked as if she was signaling, beckoning me to come to her. She didn't have to ask a nigga twice. I jumped out of the chair and made my way to her direction. But before I could make my arrival, I stopped by the kitchen. I grabbed a bowl and threw in some strawberries, pineapples, and blueberries. After washing them off, I went into the room.

"I was wondering when you were going to make your presence known," Alani told me, never breaking eye contact as she continued playing with her pussy.

EllaSoul Productions

"I had a whole night planned for you girl. You just couldn't wait, could you?" I asked her playfully.

"Nope, so bring your yellow ass over here," she said sitting up, trying her hardest to sound demanding.

"No and lay your ass back down – tonight is all about you," I said moving further into the room. La'La laid back onto the bed, obliging my request while still staring intently into my eyes.

I grabbed her legs, pulling her to the edge of the bed and smelled her pussy. She always smelled so sweet and clean, to the point you would think that they came up with the names of perfumes after her.

I grabbed a strawberry from the bowl, dipped it in her pussy, and brought it to her mouth to taste. She ate the whole thing and smiled at me. We repeated the process three more times before I stopped.

I grabbed five blueberries out of the bowl.

"I'm about to stuff these in you. If I can get them all out using only my tongue, you gotta buy me a new car," I said laughing.

"And if you don't, what do I get?" She asked, smiling devilishly.

"Your pussy ate," I laughed, placing the blueberries inside her then going in.

210

Alani started squirming to the point that I had to hold her legs to keep her in place.

"One," I said after I removed one blueberry. "Two…"

"Damn Bae, I'm about to cum," she moaned like I cared about that shit.

"Three, four," I said snaking my tongue around her opening trying to spell my name on her shit.

"Bae, I'm almost there," she said grabbing the back of my head, holding me in place.

I moved her hands and said, "Five," while spitting the last blueberry out.

Almost simultaneously, she squirted directly in my face.

"Oops, I'm sorry bae. Can you forgive me? I'm a squirter but you knew that already," she said trying to get up. I grabbed her and unbuckled my Robin jeans at the same time, letting them fall to the floor.

"Oh, so you wanna play huh?" I asked her, pulling my ten and a half inches out of my boxers, while flipping her over.

I rammed my dick into her already wet pussy and proceeded to beat her back in.

211

"Oh fuck, I'm sorry baby," Alani moaned out.

"What happened to all that shit you was talking earlier?" I asked her pounding into her relentlessly.

"Oh shit daddy, right there," she moaned, instead of responding.

"Right where," I asked her, slapping her ass.

"Nigga right there! I'm going to slap you if you move," she growled, screaming out.

"Say no more," I responded.

Once she came, I tried to flip her over to her side, but she had other plans. She turned around, slipped my dick between her lips without even touching it. La'La's pussy was the shit, but her head game was out of this world.

"Damn Ma, just like that," I said grabbing her head.

Alani deep throated my shit and almost made me moan out like a little bitch. It was already bad enough I was standing in the middle of our bed while she was kneeling down in front of me.

"Damn girl stop that shit," I growled while she massaged my balls, taking turns sucking them.

All that extra shit she was doing was feeling too good and I didn't want to bust prematurely. I tried pushing her off, but it was like she latched on.

"Ahh fuck," I grunted feeling, my nut building. She must've felt it too because she started sucking my dick like her life depended on it. She started humming on my shit and I could've sworn I saw the pearly gates.

I didn't want to bust in her mouth, but she wouldn't let go. When I released my seeds down her throat, it felt like my dick was massaging her tonsils. Baby girl swallowed it all without missing a beat.

I turned her around and beat her shit up all night. We laid in bed spent and her hair was plastered to her face. She sweated that shit all out, but she would be alright; I'd pay for her to get it fixed again.

"I'm hungry, baby," Alani whined into my ear.

"Well I did fix you dinner, before you ruined my plans," I told her laughing.

"Well let's go eat," she responded getting out of bed and throwing on one of my t-shirts.

Our food was still in the warmer, so I just made us some plates and sat down at the table I'd set for us to have dinner at.

"This looks good," Alani commented before bowing her head to recite her prayers.

When she was done, she dug in without missing a beat. There wasn't much I loved more than a woman that could eat. I didn't want a salad, crouton, and a glass of water eating bitch that was trying to be cute. In my eyes, Alani was the epitome of a real woman, and I would never do anything that would jeopardize our life together. We complete each other, and this was only the start to a long and prosperous life together.

Chapter 47

Khanna

I laid around the house playing with my nephew, KJ, and looked up into his familiar eyes. I'd been keeping him a few days out the week for my brother since his hoe ass mother had been MIA. KJ was such a happy baby.

I rubbed my barely noticeable belly thinking of my own unborn baby. Initially, I never wanted kids. I didn't want to end up like my mother, alone and sad all the time because I gave a part of my body to somebody that didn't deserve me. I also didn't want to have my kids suffer because of the poor decisions one or both of their parents had made.

Children are innocent, and I didn't want to end up being a fucked-up mother to mine. Then, with the way that Dae and I argued, I didn't want him or her in a toxic environment. But since being around my nephew so much, I'd been looking at the thought of being a mother totally differently. I was now excited to know that I had a little bundle growing inside of me that would soon be a whole human being. I think the entire process is fascinating.

Dae'Sean must've knocked my ass up as soon as we got back together. Shit between us had gotten better since we brought all of our indiscretions to the

215

light. He came home at a decent hour, he hadn't had any bitches calling his phone all hours of the night, and we ate dinner together every night. I just hoped we could stay like this. They say when something usually felt too good to be true, it usually was. Dae'Sean had even gone as far as to cut his personal phone off at night and only kept on his business phone.

I picked KJ up to place him inside of his pack and play so that I could make us some lunch. He just started giggling and laughing, which in turn caused me to smile.

When Khan Jr. first came out, he looked just like my brother and I. But the more I looked at him now, he was starting to look like Brooke except for his eyes. He didn't have Khan's eyes or Brooke's eyes, but they looked so familiar.

I shrugged it off and proceeded to make us something to eat. While I was cutting up the chicken for my salad, I heard my phone ringing. I picked up and it was Alani. We'd been getting pretty cool over the months.

"What's up, Girly?" I answered.

"Shit, chilling. I might need you to ride out with me," she stated. That made me wonder where the hell Bam was. She was taking a little longer to warm up to me than Alani did, but we were at least cordial with each other.

216

As if she'd read my mind, she said, "I don't know where the hell Bam is. Her ass has been MIA."

"I don't mind, but I got KJ with me right now and I don't know where Khan's ass is," I told her.

"Well bring him and we can drop him off at my mother's house. She has Karizma too, anyways," she told me.

"Alright hoe, I'm on my way," I told her hanging up the phone.

I checked on lil' Khan and, seeing that he was asleep, I went to go get dressed in all black. I already knew what Alani meant by ride out. I threw on some black joggers with a long-sleeved black shirt and black Timberlands. Then, I grabbed my Glock nine that Khan had bought for me and I carried with me everywhere. I dressed KJ and packed him a bag with formula, cereal, oatmeal, plenty of diapers, and three changes of clothes. I had so much of his stuff at my house that I eventually just turned one of my guest rooms into his room.

When I made it to Alani's house, she was walking out of the door as soon as I was pulling into her driveway. She was dressed in attire similar to mine, only she had on a black tee shirt and black leggings. She hopped into the passenger seat and looked back at the baby.

217

"He's so cute. It's hard to believe that he's Brooke's son," she said with a hint of sadness in her voice.

I know I didn't like her at first, but I know that this girl really loved my brother. Shit, she probably still did judging by how she was staring at his son. Love doesn't just die overnight, but I didn't blame her for finally leaving him. He'd done too much foul shit to her and the average bitch would have left him a long time ago. Alani was built Ford tough, so when she said she had reached her breaking point, you knew shit between them had gotten bad.

"Back out and make a right," she said, turning around and staring out the window.

As she gave me the directions to her mother's house, I also reflected as I assumed she was doing. I just wanted my family to be happy. Being that Alani and Bam were my family through Rock and Khan, I want them to be happy as well. Especially since me and Dae were in a good head space. I knew that there was a time when I played a part in ruining Alani's life and constantly tried to break her and my brother up, but now she was who I wanted him to be with. She had always been down for him and she's a really good person at heart.

But I had a bird-brained bitch in my ear blabbing on about wanting to be in a relationship with my brother and for some reason, I felt like they would be a good fit together. Brooke was my best bitch at the time, so why wouldn't I feel like she was the woman for my brother? I didn't know Alani from a can of beans then, but she had what one would call chronic bitch face. At any given time of the day, it would look like she had an attitude out of this world. She always looked mean, so I instantly didn't like her.

"Pull into this drive way right here," she said when we got to a gated community called Lafayette Shores, right in the heart of Norfolk.

She made sure her mama was in a place that ensured she would be hard to touch. If only I could get my mama to move, but every time that Khan and I brought it up, she always says, "I ain't no damn punk and there ain't never been an ounce of pussy in my blood. If somebody wants to run up in this bitch and pull some fuck shit, they gone be in for a rude awakening because I definitely got some hot shit with their name on it and I'mma put it right in their ass."

"I'll be right back," La'La said, getting out.

She went to the back door and grabbed KJ's carrier and baby bag, taking him into the house. She came out only few minutes later and with that, we were off. I didn't even bother to ask how she'd convinced her mom to watch her soon-to-be Ex-

219

Husband's love child, but what I did know was it couldn't have been me. Ain't no way in hell that I would agree to do some shit like that. You couldn't even pay me to watch a child that was conceived on infidelity.

When we got to our destination, it looked a little familiar, but I couldn't remember where I knew it from until we got inside: we were in Brooke's old house.

"Bitch, what the fuck are we doing here?" I whispered to Alani.

"I need some answers and I need them now. I've let this smut slide for far too long. If you ain't got the balls to help me, you can go now," she sneered back.

I didn't say anything else as I followed her to the master bedroom. We heard the shower running and Brooke's non-singing ass in there singing *25 reasons* by Nivea. Alani's ole thug ass crept in the bathroom with me hot on her heels and snatched back the shower curtain.

"I can't help but wonder if you're singing about my husband," Alani said with death in her eyes.

Brooke's nasty naked sloppy body made my stomach turn. I knew I wasn't a skinny bitch, but I was in the gym a minimum of three days a week to at least keep my shit toned up. I didn't have any cellulite dripping down my thighs, either. I'm thick, but I work hard to keep my shit together.

Brooke stood there looking like a dumb deer caught in the head lights. Without waiting for her to respond, Alani punched Brooke in her head knocking her slam out. I didn't even notice she had put on brass knuckles.

"Help me get her to the car," Alani said looking at me.

"Who said I wanted to put this bitch in my shit? Dae'Sean just bought me that damn Infinity," I snapped.

I wished my simple ass would've asked her where we were going first, then I would've been better prepared. I could've at least grabbed my old Toyota.

"Bitch, I told you when we got here if you ain't want to do it then you could leave, but you chose to stay. So, like I said, help me put her in the car. I'll pay to get yo' shit detailed and the whole nine," she told me while attempting to wrap Brooke in the shower curtain.

"Are you going to get it waxed, too?" I asked her grinning.

221

"YES Khanna, damn! Now help me get this sloppy ass hoe up, with your fucking spoiled ass. I don't see how Megan and Khan put up with your ass," she huffed.

"Say no more," I responded and started helping her out

That was all I needed to hear. I didn't care about none of that shit she was talking, Alani was family now, and I'm used to getting my way, so she better get used to it. My mother and brother had always gotten me whatever the fuck it was I wanted so my sister-in-law would just have to get with the program.

"Damn La'La, you couldn't have let the bitch get dressed first. Her fucking hairy ass wolf pussy is scaring me," I complained.

Alani laughed, "Girl, I promise to make it up to you. Let's just get this bitch in the car without nobody seeing us. After all, it is still broad daylight outside."

"Well nobody told yo' ass to do it in the daytime," I sassed.

"Whatever," was her only reply.

I backed my car into the driveway and we got Brooke's big ass into the trunk.

"Let's get this bitch to the warehouse before she wakes up. I didn't hit her ass that hard," she laughed again.

We hopped in the car and rode towards the warehouse. I'm actually happy she did call me because I had some questions for her sneaky, loose pussy ass too.

Chapter 48

Megan

♫ Life ain't no rehearsal the cameras always rolling ♫

"Oh shit big daddy right there," I moaned in the ear of my secret lover. I know that I shouldn't be fucking with him, but that's what makes it feel so much better. Right when he was about to bust, he pulled out and I sucked him dry.

He laid back on my bed spent.

"So, why exactly can't I see my fucking kids?" He asked me.

Yeah, you guessed it right, I'm fucking my baby daddy. Khan and Khanna thought their daddy was dead, but as you now know, he is alive and well. When my kids were young, I told them he just left us, but in reality, he had gotten into bed with some bad people. Kane made some fucked up decisions when it came down to taking care of his family.

Kane had a good as job as a landscaper and even had big dreams to open his own landscaping business. The company he was working for went under and he was laid off. He tried to find work, but nobody would hire him. Instead of coming home and telling me so that I could help him out, he started trafficking for the Milano Crime family.

One day, he got robbed for two million dollars' worth of shit. He knew they would try to kill him if he didn't produce either the drugs or the money, so he got the money from a loan shark, and fucked that up by drinking and gambling so then he had both the Milano crime family and the loan shark after him. When he finally told me about what was going on, it was too late because he was already in too deep. So, to keep them from coming after his family, he left.

After being on the run for a decade, he faked his death… silly me for thinking that he was going to come back home once it was all over. Boy, did I have it completely wrong. This nigga had gotten married and forgot all about our asses. Being that I wasn't a weak bitch, I put on my big girl drawls and kept it pushing like I had been doing. I had two kids to raise and I'd be damned if I had let the fucked-up decisions that a man made deter me from being the mother my children needed me to be.

"Nigga, first of all, get all that fucking bass out of your voice. Secondly, you are the sole reason why your kids don't fucking know you. You fucked my family up then you had the fucking nerve to go and get married on me. Nigga, fuck you. Matter of fact, get the fuck out my house! You better hope

225

your son don't kill your simple ass for the shit you've done!" I yelled.

I started swinging on his ass and throwing his clothes at him. He had some fucking nerve. How dare he act like I fucked him over in some way? Acting like I'm keeping children away from him when our kids are grown as hell. Niggas man, I swear you can't live with 'em, you can't live with 'em. The only thing that they're good for was leaving you with a wet ass and a broken heart.

When I was sure that Kane's dirty ass was out of my house, I headed to take a shower. I stepped into my bathroom and set the water to an appropriate temperature. I needed my water to be extremely hot, I mean damn near burning me. Kane's ass had life fucked up if he thought I needed his ass; I just had an itch that needed to be scratched from time to time.

I had a weird thing going on with myself. It may not make sense to others, but it made perfect sense to me. Regardless of my age, I felt like if I wanted some dick but I wasn't in a relationship. So, if I fucked somebody I'd already fucked, then I wasn't on no hoe shit. Fucking somebody that I already fucked kept my number low. Y'all know what number I'm talking about – how many bodies I got, how many miles were on my pussy, etc. Plus, I didn't want to get some new dick and it be some poo. Therefore, I'd rather get some guaranteed good

226

dick. So as long as I was fucking somebody I'd already been with, I could keep my hoe conscience clear. Fuck y'all, don't judge me.

I don't even know why I still fooled around with Kane. He did me so dirty all those years back. I know it'd been practically two decades, but my extra petty ass was still salty about it. He thought I didn't know and I was still the green bitch I was all those years ago, but I was very aware of the fact that his problems were handled long before he found his way back home to me and our very adult offspring.

I'd still been battling with myself on forgiving him. I understood him being a man and having needs, but to marry a bitch while he was on the run was a punch to the gut for me. I carried two of this man's big-headed ass children and this was how he decided to repay me – by marrying a bitch he hadn't even known all that long.

Oh well, I couldn't really dwell on that right now. In the meantime, I had to figure out a way to break it to my kids that their father was still alive. Initially when I told them that he was dead, I was under the impression that I would never see him again, but the universe had a funny way of working. In life, you tended to have to play the cards that were dealt and Kane had given me a fucked up hand.

Chapter 49

Brooke

♫ What goes up must come down ♫

I awoke with the worst headache known to man. I tried to move, but I then realized I was suspended from the ceiling by thick heavy chains. When I opened my eyes, I noticed I was in some type of building. I tried to think back to the last thing that I did, then I remembered seeing Alani and Khanna in my house. Everything else after that was a blur.

It was then that the panic started to set in. I didn't know exactly what these hoes had me in here for, but I knew it couldn't be anything good. Well, I can't exactly say that I don't know because it could be a number of things. I'd fucked both of their men and done a shitload of other sleazy shit, so I could definitely take my pick of any of those.

If they thought I was going to bow out and accept defeat, then they had another thing coming.

"Where the fuck you two stupid bitches at?" I screamed, kicking my feet back and forth. I was scared shitless of what they might do to me, but I'll be damned if I showed them the fear that resonated within me.

228

"Speak your muthafucking piece. Let's air all this dirty laundry out now!" I yelled when my first outburst received no response.

I continued to kick my feet, but eventually stopped. The chains around my wrists were so tight and being that they were supporting all of my weight, they'd started cutting into my wrists. Even though I was no longer trying to move, my bodyweight weighing on the chains continued to cut into me. I watched as the blood dripped down my arms in the dimly lit room.

I knew that I had done a lot of fucked up shit to people in my life, but I refused for this to be the way that I went out. I didn't want to just sit here and bleed out. Instead, I used this time to think of some of the decisions I'd made in life thus far. Now, I didn't always have the best of judgment, but I didn't think I'd done enough damage to make them want to kill me.

I guess some people really took you knowingly fucking their man to heart. Kanye shrugs. I couldn't do anything about that shit now. Every time I tried to turn my life around, that shit didn't work. It's like the devil was behind me with that hot stick.

I made an honest attempt to be a better person but loving the wrong man had always been my downfall. Not only was Khan the wrong man for

229

me, but he was also somebody else's man. When I found out that they were in a serious relationship, I should've laid off of him, but I just couldn't fathom him being with somebody other than me. It may not seem like it, but I really do have a big heart, and when I love, I love hard.

I just gave all of the love that I had in me to a man that not only didn't deserve it but didn't even want it. Khan told me time and time again that he didn't want a relationship out of me but being a fool in love made me disregard all of that shit.

I would accept some of the responsibility for the situation that I ended up in, but Khan also played a huge part in it. What men failed to realize was that if a woman was in love with him, but he expressed that he didn't look at her like that, or his feelings weren't mutual, women would continue to hold onto the hope that they would one day come around. Every time Khan bedded me, even though he told me that nothing was going to come from us, he enabled me to become more attached to him.

Women would rather settle for a piece of a man that they loved or were in love with, than to have to live without them completely. It sounded foolish from the outside looking in, but you had to be lost in a situation of that nature to fully understand. I was just a victim of circumstance.

230

My mind quickly shot to my baby boy. I tried my hardest to do right by him. People wanted to constantly fuck me over, especially his father. That nigga didn't give a fuck about anybody but his damn self. He pushed me damn near to the brink of insanity and KJ was what brought me back. I pictured my chubby cheeked baby while my body got weak from the amount of blood I was losing. I managed to lift my head enough from the resting position on my chest to look down and see a small puddle of blood forming below me.

I had underestimated these bitches. It was nothing but pure torture to allow somebody to die slowly, especially without as much as a word. I made a silent promise to myself and my son that in my next life, I would give a good 'ole college try at doing better in life.

At least I can rest easy knowing that my son is in good hands with his father, I thought as everything faded to black.

EllaSoul Productions

Chapter 50

Khan

I got a call from Alani saying it was an emergency. I immediately thought something was wrong with Karizma until she told me to meet her at the warehouse. Then I remembered that Karizma was at Alani's mother's house. La'La hadn't put in any work since she got pregnant, so I was curious as to why she was even there. Not that I was mad or anything, because regardless of what ever had gone on in our personal lives, we had always put business first. So, I knew that whatever reason she had to be up there was a good one.

I pulled up to the warehouse at the same time as Rich's bitch ass. I was baffled about why Khanna's car was there, but I guess I would found out shortly, especially when she was the one who had my son.

"What the fuck you doing here, my nigga?" I questioned him.

We were very strategic in picking the location that we operated from, so it was really rubbing me the wrong way for a nigga that I didn't fuck with to know where I held a lot of my artillery. Most of my workers didn't even know where this specific location was. When we conducted our meetings, they were held in a warehouse on the other side of town.

232

"Nigga ain't no reason to get all swole, I'm just trying to figure out the same fucking thing."

Instead of dignifying him with a response, I led the way into the warehouse. Somebody who didn't know where they were going would never find the entrance. We'd it built into the wall in a way that the naked eye couldn't see, unless you knew what you were looking.

"Wait right here homeboy," I told him, holding my arm out to keep him from walking any further.

Once I opened the door, I signaled for him proceed. The first room that we walked into was the room that we used as a conference room for our smaller meetings which only consisted of the most trusted and loyal workers.

I led the way down the hallway looking for La'La. When I made it to our joint office in very back of the building, I saw La'La and Khanna eating hot wings, pizza, and drinking Pepsi. They sat there laughing like they were best friends and Kevin Hart had just told them the funniest joke they'd ever heard.

"Bout time y'all made it. Y'all hungry?" La'La asked, holding up a box of pizza.

"What the fuck y'all doing here lounging around like this the fucking Taj Mahal? More importantly, why are we here and where is KJ?" I asked, growing irritated with this whole situation.

"Well as you both may know, I was shot by an unknown subject. I had an idea as who may have done it but was not completely sure. So, with that being said, we are here today to get to the bottom of it all," she said pointing to the monitors that they were sitting in front of. "And KJ is at my mom's spot along with Kay-Kay," she added.

We had cameras on every inch of the building with not one blind spot anywhere. I walked towards the monitors with Rich hot on my heels. I'm guessing he was just as curious as I was, if not more. I didn't know who I was going to see, but I wasn't surprised at who it was. Brooke was always my top suspect, I just hadn't been able to find her since I took my son from her.

She was in one of the three rooms that we had set up for torture. She was hanging from the ceiling with blood covering the entire front of her body. The bitch didn't even look like she was alive. As if she was reading my mind, Alani spoke up.

"I gave her a shot of some shit that I got from my nigga, Science, to thicken her blood so she won't bleed out."

Damn, I thought to myself, *she didn't leave one stone unturned.*

234

As I continued to look at the monitors, I started having mixed emotions. Not that I loved Brooke or anything, but I had mad love for her because she's the mother of my child.

"Well boys, let's get this show on the road," my sister said standing up.

I didn't know what Alani said or did to Khanna, but she was a totally different person right now. I just shook my head as we all walked out of the room towards the torture chamber that Brooke was being held in. Taking the lead, Khanna walked over to a table in the corner and grabbed some smelling salts. She then headed over to Brooke while we all stood back and watched. Khanna snapped the smelling salts under her nose causing her head to snap up.

"Remember me, bitch?" Khanna asked, punching Brooke in her face as soon as she became alert. "So, here's how this is going to go. I'm going to ask you a series of questions and I want the truth, the whole truth, and nothing but the truth so help YOU God," she said lowering the chains slightly so that they were eye to eye.

"Shoot then," Brooke said groggily with her voice slightly slurring.

"First, I want to know why you fucked Dae'Sean," Khanna asked her.

235

"You said you want the truth, right? Okay so here it goes. You kept bragging about how good and big his dick was and I wanted to see for myself. And boy was it even better than you described. Lawd have mercy on my soul, because I'm about to cum again just thinking about how he ate my pussy from the back just like you described. He a nasty nigga Khanna, you should leave him," Brooke said laughing.

She must have struck some kind of nerve because Khanna picked up a Taser from the table and zapped Brooke's ass. She started squirming around until Khanna let go.

"How you gone ask me a question then get mad at the answer that I give you? That's what's wrong with you females these days; always asking for answers to questions that you ain't mentally prepared to hear."

Instead of responding to her, Khanna continued, "Second question, who shot my sister?"

This was the million-dollar question here.

"Shoot somebody? I don't even own a gun," Brooke said staring Khanna right in her eyes.

"Wrong answer, hoe," she replied zapping her ass again.

Brooke hollered out in pain. Alani took this as her cue to step forward.

"So, what you are trying to tell me is you don't know who tried to kill me and failed but succeeded in killing my unborn child?"

"Aww, you were pregnant? Sorry to hear that but you bitches did try to kill my son, by the grace of God he survived. And… since you and Khan are not together, it must have been this fine ass nigga's baby. Damn, he can get it. He looks like he has a big dick too, probably bigger than yours, Khan. Tell me La'La, between the two of them, whose dick is bigger?" Brooke asked mischievously.

La'La and Khanna just started raining blow after blow to her face and body. They busted her lip and I swear I heard a rib crack, and Brooke could do nothing but hang there and take it.

Rich, who had been silent the entire time, finally spoke up, "Enough."

He walked in their direction and stopped directly in front of Brooke.

"Why do you have to have such an ugly personality? I might have to let you taste the family jewels," he said grabbing his crotch.

La'La shot him the death stare but I cleared my throat signaling for her to chill out. Brooke had

237

bad blood with everybody in this room with the exception of Rich. Maybe he'd be the nigga that actually got some real answers out of her ass.

La'La walked over in my direction and I whispered in her ear, "Let's see how this pans out. She has no problem with Rich like she does the rest of us. He just might be able get into her head and find out some shit that she won't tell us. I'm also curious to see how he'll handle himself," I told her with a smirk.

She just mugged me and walked away. I could do nothing but chuckle at her lil' mad, sexy ass.

Chapter 51

Rich

I saw the way Brooke looked at me with lust filled eyes, so I decided I was going to use it to our advantage. The bitches never really could resist a nigga like me. From my smooth blemish free brown skin, to the few tattoos that I had strategically placed on my torso and neck, to my swag, and the charisma that eludes from my persona, I have to beat bitches off my dick on a daily.

But I couldn't do my lady like that. Alani is the type of female that can definitely make and nigga a one-woman man… well, with the exception of Khan's ass. The look on Brooke's face leads me to believe that I can get her ass to do whatever I want with promises of letting her taste the soul pole.

"Lower me down and I'll show you why your boy over there couldn't get enough of me," Brooke said while trying to look as seductive as she possibly could with blood covering eighty percent of her body. I stroked the side of her of her face "Look love, this how this is going to work. You are going to tell me whatever you think is credible information. Then, I'm going to find out if it's legit. Then if I find that you aren't on any bull shit, and I do mean IF, you just might get to walk out of here with your life. Do you understand me?" I asked her seriously.

"Anything for you daddy," Brooke purred making my stomach churn. She should have oinked because she looks just like a fucking pig. "Just don't disappoint me and make me regret doing this for you," I told her looking directly into her eyes. I lowered her to the ground and Khan came and escorted her into a room containing nothing but a small mattress with a pillow and a thin ass sheet, and a bathroom.

"So is this my cell, Khan?" She asked turning to Khan.

"Just a little quality assurance," he replied smugly.

"Fuck you," she yelled in his face.

"Never again bitch," he countered.

Sick of their back and forth I replied "We'll be back to talk to you later. In the meantime, clean yourself up."

When we got back to the office, Alani said "Don't get fucked up" while Khanna shot me the death stare. They walked past us out the warehouse and Khanna made it her business to bump me while leaving out. I just sighed and shook my head. I guess this is the thanks I get for helping out.

Chapter 52

Alani

After leaving the warehouse with Khanna in tow, I was a little tight with Rich. I willed myself not to get too mad considering that he helped us out a great deal. We probably could've tortured Brooke all night and still wouldn't have gotten any answers.

I headed to my mother's house so that we could pick up the kids but I kept getting a funny feeling in the pit of my stomach. If Khan ever taught me anything, it was to trust my gut. I checked my rearview and didn't see anything suspicious nor did it appear that anybody was following us, but I still couldn't seem to shake this feeling.

"Khanna, call Khan and tell him to meet us at my mother's house."

She called Khan and I pulled out my phone to call Rich.

"Meet me at my mama's house," I told him.

"Locked and loaded?" he asked me.

"And you know it, boo," I replied and then hung up.

"What's going on, sis?" Khanna asked me.

"I just got a funny feeling that some shit is about to go down," I told her, checking my Glock while I was still driving.

"Say no more," she replied making sure her nine was fully loaded with one in the chamber.

We drove in silence the remainder of the way to my mom's. The closer we got to her house, the more uneasy I felt. If something happened to my mother, I was sure to go berserk. When we pulled up, her house dark as shit. The rest of the street was lit up by the street lights, but it seemed as if her house had a dark cloud looming over it. It stood out to me because she usually always has her porch light on.

I got out the car and made sure I was strapped with all my toys. I had my hunting knife, a box cutter, a stun gun, my Glock 17, my .357, and my Ruger. As skimpy as my attire appeared, you never would guess I was sporting so much artillery.

I signaled to Khanna to follow my lead as we walked up the steps to her front door. I was going to use my key until the door opened on its own. I now knew for sure that something is up. It didn't matter that she lived in a middle-class neighborhood now, I grew up in the 'hood. I knew my old lady would never leave her door unlocked and open.

We stepped into the house with our straps out. The house was eerily quiet for her to have two babies in there.

Maybe she's put them to bed already, I thought to myself trying to stay positive.

But I really could only think the worst and everything was leading me to believe that something isn't kosher.

Once we cleared the first floor, we made our way up to the second. I checked all the rooms except Karizma's room, saving that one for last. When I got to Karizma's room door, my heart rate quickened. I pushed the door completely open and almost fainted. It was a fucking bloody massacre. I spotted my mother laying on the floor by Kay's crib.

I rushed to her side to make sure she was still breathing, and she was, thank God. Khanna pulled out her phone to call the ambulance. Angeline Clarke was one of the sweetest women in the world. I just couldn't wrap my head around the fact that somebody would want to hurt her. Then it hit me. Where the fuck were the kids?

I checked my mom from head to toe but there was so much blood I couldn't tell how many times she was hit, but I knew that she was shot from the shells on the floor.

"Ma, hold on. I got some help coming," I told her while I rocked her back and forth, crying.

"I tried to stop her La," my mother struggled to say. "Shhh, don't talk," I said bending down to kiss her forehead.

"She took them, I tried to stop her but I couldn't," she said.

"Who was it Mommy?" I asked her.

"She told me to tell you that she would be in touch. I'm sorry, La'La. I love you," was the last thing my mother said before her eyes rolled back and she went limp.

I let out a blood curdling scream before everything faded to black.

EllaSoul Productions

Chapter 53

Erica

I bet you all are wondering who I am. Well, allow me to introduce myself. My name is Erica Catalina May and it has been me wreaking havoc on Khan's life and the lives of everybody that is associated with him.

I thought that he was different at first because he treated me really well, showering me with gifts and making sure that I wanted for nothing. Imagine my surprise when he walked into my job, Heavenly Touch, and paid handsomely for his soon-to-be wife and her best friend to get pampered for an engagement party/birthday party.

I tried my best to be cordial when she came in to my job, but it was killing me not to take her out. It felt as if I was in a bad dream, no fuck that, a nightmare that I wouldn't be waking up from anytime soon. The man that I grew to love and whom treated me like a queen, had a whole family outside of his "relationship" with me.

I had no idea he even had a girlfriend, so I was crushed when I found out about their relationship. Being sheltered as a child to the city, I had no idea that he was the big man in town alongside his girl, Alani. I thought maybe he'd met someone new and was going to eventually call to break things off with me. But upon further

245

investigation, I uncovered that they'd been together for years. She may not have done anything to me personally, but she's guilty by association.

With tears in my eyes, I rubbed Khan's daughter Karizma's hair. She looked just like her daddy. It made me wonder what our baby would look like if he'd allowed me to deliver to term. That's right, I'd had two abortions during a six-month relationship. He fed me a bullshit story about not being ready for kids, only for me to later find out that he had three children on the way by three different women. Obviously, he didn't make any of them get an abortion.

KJ started stirring in his sleep, so I started to pat his back to keep him from waking up completely. I just wanted to take the kids and be on my way. I'd convinced myself that they were mine and that Khan was keeping them from me. I followed Alani from her house to her mom's and waited until I felt the time was right.

I'd bought a gun from some lil' stick up kid even though I had no plans on using it at first. I had my own gun but, in the event, that I had to use one, I didn't want anything to be able to trace back to me. One of Khan's baby mama's got a new car, so when I stole her old one, she didn't even bother to file a police report.

EllaSoul Productions

I followed La'La and Rich to an expensive steakhouse where they had reservations and paid one of the waiters to signal to me when they were about to leave. When I saw them waiting for the valet to bring their ride around, I took that as my cue to strike. My father used to take me to the gun range all the time when growing up, so I was definitely a good shot.

I didn't wait around after I saw her hit the ground. I thought I'd successfully taken her out only to find out later on that she'd survived. I dressed up as a nurse at the hospital she was being serviced in and tried to finish her off, but problems arose when I observed her room being guarded like Fort Knox. When that plan failed, I used my disguise to read her medical records. I smiled a little on the inside when I read that one of the bullets I delivered to her body killed a baby that she was carrying. Serves her right since her husband killed two of mine. Like I'd said before, she's guilty by association.

I could never get close enough to permanently remove Alani from the picture, so I decided to go after the children that were rightfully mine. I didn't want to hurt anybody's mother, but in war, there are casualties. This was definitely war now since Khan deemed it necessary to fuck with my feelings the way he had.

I wouldn't have shot the old lady had she not come into the room when she did. Then, instead of

247

just letting me leave with my kids, she wanted to play super human and try her hand at keeping them from me. All she had to do was let me walk out the door with them.

I had plans to bring Khan down to his knees, starting with his children. He was going to miss them, but I didn't care.

They are rightfully mine, anyway.

To be continued

EllaSoul Productions